Simon Brett OBE was educated at Dulwich College and Wadham College, Oxford, where he gained a First Class Honours Degree in English. A former radio and television producer, he has to date written over ninety books. A great many are crime novels, including the Charles Paris, Mrs Pargeter and Fethering series.

Simon was Chairman of the Crime Writers Association from 1986 to 1987 and of the Society of Authors from 1995 to 1997. He is President of the Detection Club and was awarded the 2014 CWA Diamond Dagger. He lives near Arundel in West Sussex and is married with grown-up children, three grandsons, one granddaughter and a cat called Polly. In 2016 he was awarded an OBE for services to literature.

9030 00006 9597 4

Also by Simon Brett

Blotto, Twinks and the Intimate Revue

Simon Brett

Constable
An imprint of
Little, Brown Book Group
Carmelite House
50 Victoria Embankment
London EC4Y 0DZ

An Hachette UK Company
www.hachette.co.uk

CONSTABLE

CONSTABLE

First published in Great Britain in 2018 by Constable
This paperback edition published in 2019 by Constable

1 3 5 7 9 10 8 6 4 2

Copyright © Simon Brett, 2018

The moral right of the author has been asserted.

*All characters and events in this publication, other than
those clearly in the public domain, are fictitious,
and any resemblance to real persons,
living or dead, is purely coincidental.*

A CIP catalogue record for this book is available
from the British Library.

ISBN: 978-1-47212-827-0

Typeset in Palatino by Photoprint, Torquay
Printed and bound in Great Britain by Clays Ltd, Elcograf S.p.A.

Papers used by Constable are from well-managed forests and
other responsible sources.

MIX
Paper from

To the George Writers

Boring Old London

Blotto didn't really like London. As Devereux Lyminster, younger brother to the Duke of Tawcester, living in the idyllic setting of Tawcester Towers in the county of Tawcestershire, everything he needed in life was right there on his doorstep. The estate had its own cricket pitch and that, with forays to other grounds, kept him ecstatically occupied during the summer months. In the winter, nothing made him happier than sitting astride his magnificent hunter Mephistopheles, thundering in pursuit of foxes and devastating the fields of the local farmers. And all through the year, he enjoyed belting along the narrow lanes of Tawcestershire in his blue Lagonda, scattering the peasantry on to the verges and into the ditches of the county. (In this he was merely obeying ancestral instinct. Families like the Lyminsters had a long tradition of mutilating serfs.)

Blotto was a man of simple pleasures and simple mind. Who needed London?

His sister Twinks, properly known as Honoria Lyminster, was a woman of more sophisticated tastes. She was also a woman of astonishing intellect and remarkable beauty. The effect of this latter quality could be measured by the number of men who fell for her like fainting guardsmen. Few of the male gender had been constructed with sufficient resistance to withstand the allure of her slender frame, white-blonde hair and azure eyes. Twinks was so inured to hearing daily declarations of love that her invariable response – 'Don't talk such toffee' – had become an instinct to her. It was not that she didn't find men physically attractive. It was just that she encountered so few who came even near to being her intellectual equals.

So, although she enjoyed many country pursuits, and although she could always engage her brainpower with some project like translating Dostoyevsky into Sanskrit, Twinks required the stimulus of London far more than her brother did. If a couple of weeks went by without a visit to the capital, she would begin to get a little twitchy, and a month of uninterrupted Tawcester Towers life would find her bouncing off its ancestral walls.

Though he didn't welcome them, Blotto was no longer surprised when his sister accosted him with the ominous words, 'Blotters me old frying pan, could I have a wordette with you . . . ?' He knew all too well what they would lead to.

On this latest occasion, on a perfect English summer's morning, he had just been down to the garage to watch as his chauffeur Corky Froggett finished polishing the Lagonda, and was on his way to set the world to rights in the stables by communing with Mephistopheles, when Twinks cornered him in the Long Rose Walk and asked the familiar question.

'Blotto me old frying pan, could I have a wordette with you . . . ?'

'Erm . . . Well . . . Tickey-Tockey,' her brother responded uneasily.

'Fact is, the Tawcester Towers Hunt Ball is on the horizon,' she went on.

'Well, I'll be snickered,' said Blotto, feigning surprise. In fact, he knew full well what she was talking about. For him Hunt Balls – even when held on home turf – were ghastly

2

blots on the social calendar. His idea of a good time didn't include dancing. Though so elegant at the crease in a cricket match, in a foxtrot Blotto was all left feet. Also Hunt Balls brought with them the recurring hazard of beautiful and wealthy debutantes wanting to marry him. So far, he had managed to escape the manacles of matrimony, but he knew it was only a matter of time before his mother, the craggy and redoubtable Dowager Duchess of Tawcester, dictated that he should twiddle the old marital reef knot. And he knew that mothers of eligible young girls would already be circling in preparation for showing off their wares at Tawcester Towers.

For these and other reasons, Blotto would always rather be immersed in cold custard than go to a Hunt Ball.

He waited in some trepidation for what his sister would say next.

It came. 'And my wardrobe's as empty as a policeman's imagination. Just got the maid to lay out the contents in my boudoir – nothing there that doesn't scream "so last year" at the volume of a stuck pig. I'm afraid, Blotters me old tub of tooth powder, an assault raid on the London couturiers is the absolute Wellington command.'

Broken biscuits, Blotto murmured inwardly, which was a measure of his discomfiture. He was not in the habit of using strong language. But all he said audibly was, 'Good ticket, Twinks me old bowl of shaving soap. Then let us unleash the old Lag at worm's waking in the morning, and pongle up to London.'

It was not in Blotto's nature to be cast down for long. Within seconds, his customary sunny disposition had emerged from behind the clouds. When he came to think about it, London wasn't such a treacle tin after all. While Twinks was off consulting her needle-wielders, he had ways of filling the time. The Savoy did a decent enough breakfast, luncheon at one of his clubs, early evening bite at a supper club, take in a few giggles at the latest intimate

3

revue, and round off the metropolitan day with a large dinner somewhere. He could cope with that.

And, after all, it would only be for a couple of days.

A summons to visit the Dowager Duchess of Tawcester in the Blue Morning Room never boded well. Blotto and Twinks's redoubtable mother was built from the primordial rock which predated the Age of the Dinosaurs (though they were in fact a species with which she shared many characteristics). Her upbringing of her three children (the oldest, universally known as Loofah, was the current Duke) had not involved any modish frills like proximity or affection, but her presence still loomed over the entire Tawcester Towers estate.

Blotto had always been appropriately cowed by his mother. Though famously brave in the cricket and hunting fields, though unflinching in battle (particularly when facing impossible odds), the flicker of a disapproving eyebrow from his mother could still reduce him to the consistency of consommé. Blotto had always known his place when it came to women – he was undoubtedly their inferior – but nowhere was this more applicable than in his relationship with his mother. In her presence, Blotto was more cowed than a Texan cattle ranch.

Even Twinks, who had intense bravery, dazzling intellect and gender on her side, trod warily around the Dowager Duchess.

'It has come to my attention,' the old lady boomed that morning in the Blue Morning Room, 'that the two of you are planning a trip to the Metropolis.'

'Yes, Mater,' said Twinks, defiance already in her tone, as if she were expecting opposition. 'I need to tog up with some new shimmeries for the forthcoming Hunt Ball. My wardrobe's as empty as a pauper's pocket.'

The expected disagreement did not materialise. Instead, Twinks was confronted with that rare commodity from her mother – enthusiasm. 'Cracking good idea,' said the Dowager Duchess. 'Any such investment is to be recommended.'

'Investment?' echoed Twinks warily.

'Of course. The Tawcester Towers plumbing is in need of refurbishment.' The words were spoken as by a judge who had just put on his black cap, prior to passing a death sentence.

'Oh, not again, Mater! That really is a rat in the larder.'

Blotto nodded in sympathy. The precarious health of the Tawcester Towers plumbing was something of which both siblings had been aware from the nursery onward. The bronchial wheezing in its pipes had been a leitmotif to their growing up. They had become used to the thin trickles of cold brown water from taps in the great house's few bathrooms. They were used to the sounds of dripping and the smell of seepage. And their constant drinking of water from its old pipes had inoculated them forever against the effects of lead poisoning.

Blotto and Twinks had also grown up witnessing frequent attempts to improve the state of the Tawcester Towers plumbing. Recurrent floods, running down through the storeys of the old house, had prompted frequent emergency repairs, none of which did much to alleviate the basic problem of the system's antiquity. Its ravenous maw swallowed down money as a whale does krill. And on more than one occasion, the aristocratic siblings had been forced to undertake hazardous but lucrative adventures with a view to replenishing the family coffers and meeting their plumbing bills.

'It's important that you look your best,' said the Dowager Duchess ominously.

Twinks, whose brain was one of the most efficient in human history, quickly realised how her mother's enthusiasm for new Hunt Ball dresses was connected to the Tawcester Towers plumbing. Even Blotto, whose brain was one of the least efficient in human history, had a pretty fair idea of what was going on. The Mater was match-making again. It might be thought that nothing could enhance his sister's already perfect looks, but a new dress couldn't do any harm. And might prove sufficiently alluring as a bait for some vapid young man from a wealthy family to marry her and sort out the Tawcester Towers plumbing for good.

Blotto looked across at his sister with sympathy. That sympathy, though, was mixed with another emotion: relief. If the Mater was focusing her matrimonial ambitions on Twinks, then he might be let off the hook for a while.

But, even while the hope was forming in his mind, it was instantly dashed, as the Dowager Duchess continued, 'And, of course, Blotto, you always look your best at balls. So much simpler for the male of the species, isn't it? Put a monkey in evening dress and it'd pass muster, wouldn't it? We may have to put in a bit of work on your conversation, though.'

'Oh?' said Blotto feebly. 'Why?'

'Because,' his mother replied imperturbably, 'there is someone I have invited to our Hunt Ball on whom it is very important that you make an impression.'

Biscuits broken in a thousand pieces, Blotto murmured inwardly. Though, of course, he would never have allowed his mother to hear him using such strong language out loud.

He was well aware of what he was up against. The Dowager Duchess had a network of other Duchesses (with the occasional Countess and Marchioness), who made it their business to find out the precise details of all eligible young women who might be used as pawns in the complex strategies of matrimonial chess. They knew to a nicety the lineage and financial expectations of every aristocratic female under twenty in the British Isles. They knew which family scandals could be politely ignored, and which left a permanent stain on the family escutcheon. They knew in which family vaults the bodies were buried.

Their information went back long before the balls at

which such young debutantes were presented to the King and Queen. Members of the Dowager Duchess's beady-eyed collective scanned the Births columns of the right newspapers, already earmarking matrimonial potential among the hyphenated newborn.

Their network was as efficient as the Mafia, and far more deadly.

So Blotto had no doubt that, if his mother was lining up a potential bride for him, she would have done her research.

'Do you know the Earl of Midhurst?' asked the Dowager Duchess.

'No, I don't think I've actually met the boddo,' said her son miserably.

'Well, he committed the terrible social solecism of marrying an American.' Neither Blotto nor Twinks thought it was the moment to remind their mother that she had once contemplated sacrificing her younger son in the same way, as a solution to the Tawcester Towers plumbing problem.

'Didn't have the decency to go over and live with her there, so that people could pretend they didn't know about it. He actually flaunted her round the English social set, just as if she had breeding. And he bred from her, of course. No son and heir, though, just the one gel called Araminta. Quite the charmer, I gather. And relatively civilised. Doesn't talk with an American accent, or anything embarrassing like that.

'But, since she's a filly, what it means is that, when the Earl's clogs pop orf, title goes to some distant cousin. Only the title, though. Prior to her marriage, the so-called Countess had some legal instrument drawn up – by an American lawyer, of course, you have to go over there to get the real shysters – whereby her money is inherited by her children, *regardless of gender*.' In the Dowager Duchess's tone, disgust at such commercial foresight mixed with an undeniable element of admiration.

'Terribly bad form, of course, denying the right of

primogeniture, but here we could be talking ill winds. The gel's called Araminta fffrench-Wyndeau – and, as everyone with the proper breeding knows, the second and third *f*s in her surname are silent. Anyway, she will inherit all of her mother's wealth. And that wealth comes from *oil*!' Again, contempt for anyone whose money wasn't inherited vied with delight at the knowledge of how much of it could be generated by something as crude as oil.

'So, Blotto . . .' The Dowager Duchess fixed her implacable eye on her younger son. 'For the sake of the Lyminster family honour . . . you know what you have to do.'

'Tickey-Tockey, Mater,' came the wretched response.

'At the Hunt Ball, you must besiege Araminta fffrench-Wyndeau, you must use all of your wiles . . .'

'But I haven't got any wiles.'

'. . . any ruse . . .'

'I haven't got any ruse either . . . well, except the ones I'm wearing.'

'. . . to ensure that the gel falls for you like a peppered partridge. Anything less, on the night of the Hunt Ball, than her acceptance of your proposal, Blotto, I will regard as an abject failure on your part!'

'Good ticket, Mater,' he murmured abjectly.

2

Encounters at the Gren

On the rare occasions when Blotto had to stay in London on his own, he tended to park the old jim-jams at one of his clubs. Of these he usually favoured the Grenadiers in St James's, universally known by its members as 'the Gren'. It was one of those clubs devoted to making a young man's transition from public school to adult life as painless as possible. To this end, it employed an all-male staff, and chefs whose ambitions never aspired above the level of nursery food.

Whenever Blotto went to the Gren, he was bound to meet a few of his old muffin-toasters from Eton, whose company would guarantee a riotous evening of throwing bread rolls at ancestral portraits, galloping through the wine list, and eventual collapse in a room where his bed was the only fixed point.

When accompanied by his sister, however, he took a totally different approach. Recognising how churlish it would be for him to dine in an establishment where the footfall of a lady would have caused some half-dozen coronaries before she even made it across the foyer, he always booked them adjacent suites at the Savoy ('a boddo's always well looked after at the Savvers').

But on this particular occasion, he was granted the opportunity to have his cake (along with other nursery food) and eat it. Lunch at the Gren, an afternoon in one of its capacious leather armchairs to sleep that off, followed by dinner with Twinks at the Savvers. All creamy éclair, so far as Blotto was concerned.

Though he had done the driving (the Lagonda vied only with Mephistopheles and his cricket bat as Blotto's most treasured possession), the siblings had been accompanied to London by their chauffeur, Corky Froggett. A man of military background and impeccable loyalty, it was his earnest ambition to give his life in defence of any member of the family at Tawcester Towers, but particularly of the young master, Devereux Lyminster. The fact that this supreme sacrifice had never yet been required of him remained a constant source of disappointment to Corky Froggett. But he lived in hope.

Corky was one of those men who blossomed in wartime, and for whom peace would always come as something of a disappointment. He had excelled as a fighting machine in the 'recent little dust-up in France' and sincerely regretted that his homicidal tendencies were no longer allowed free rein. The war had also represented the high spot of his life in other respects. In France he had met a young Resistance fighter who had fulfilled his every expectation of what a woman might be. But the fortunes of war brought about an inevitable separation. Corky and his ideal woman lost touch and had no means of contacting each other. So, though he indulged in enjoyable skirmishes with many of the below-stairs beauties of Tawcester Towers, none of them could match the memory of his lost Yvette.

When Blotto brought the Lagonda to a perfect halt outside the main doors of The Savoy, it was left to Corky to park and check in their valises. Twinks hailed a cab and demanded that the driver take her to 'Madame Clothilde of Mayfair', while Blotto set off at a brisk walk in the direction of the Gren.

* * *

10

'Dippy, you poor old thimble, what's put lumps in your custard?'

Blotto's solicitous enquiry was addressed to a young man in the club's Marlborough Bar. The man's face was twisted into a rictus of pain, and his glass clearly – and shamefully in such an environment – contained nothing stronger than ginger beer.

Dippy Le Froom had been a contemporary of Blotto's at Eton. Many's the time on the cricket pitch that they had shared unbreakable partnerships, and in their studies shared more trivial games, most of which involved hurling missiles of ink-soaked blotting paper. They were close in the way only public schoolboys can be. In other words, they insulted each other a lot, hit each other a lot, bought each other a lot of drinks, and rigidly prevented their conversation from ever straying into an area that might involve feelings.

Dippy looked up at Blotto piteously. 'Yes, I am in a bit of a treacle tin,' he admitted.

'By Wilberforce, you can say that again! You look like a pig who's lost his whistle. What's up – been losing a bit on the old gee-gees?'

Even as he asked the question, Blotto knew the answer would be no. Dippy Le Froom was sole heir to the Earl of Minchinhampton. He lived so high on the hog that the only other pigs he saw were flying ones. Dippy had a house in Mayfair, built on the scale of a Tsar's Winter Palace. He had hundreds of staff and, when he was at home, all his meals were prepared by Xavier, a chef whose reputation had spread to every continent.

So Dippy could have lost thousands on the old gee-gees every day, and still not make the smallest dent in the vast fortune which he would eventually inherit. Whatever his problem might be, it certainly wasn't financial.

'No, no,' Dippy confirmed. 'Fact is, Blotto me old bootscraper, I've done something I'm not very proud of.'

'Have you, by Denzil?' said Blotto cautiously. He had a

11

nasty feeling he was about to be shoved into a gluepot of inappropriate emotions and all that rombooley.

'I'm not sure that I should really be talking about such matters in the Gren.'

'Oh, Dippy, come on! Uncage the ferrets!'

'Righty-ho, Blotters. If you're going to put the Chinese burners on me about it, I'll tell you. The fact is . . .' Dippy gulped.

Blotto couldn't stand the silence going on too long. 'It can't be that murdy,' he said.

'I've got married.'

Oh dear. It *was* that murdy. With feeling, Blotto murmured, 'Tough gorgonzola, me old pineapple.'

'Nothing against the old bride, of course. Called Poppy. Charming gel, couldn't be nicer. It's just, you know . . .' His jaw sagged like the loose elastic on a pair of rugger shorts '. . . marriage.'

'What you need in this situation, you poor old thimble, is the starchiest of stiffeners.' Blotto turned in the direction of the barman. 'What's it to be, Dippy – a quadruple brandy?'

'No, no!' His friend hastened to negate the order. 'Can't be done, I'm afraid, old man.'

'Why not, for the love of strawberries?'

'The fact is, Blotters, I can't go home to Poppy, *smelling of drink*.'

'What, does the poor little breathsapper suffer from one of those religions which doesn't allow boddoes to do anything they might enjoy?'

'No, it's worse than that.'

'I can't imagine anything being worse than that.'

'Poppy *trusts* me!'

'Trusts you not to have too much of the old alkiboodles?'

'Trusts me not to have *any* of the old alkiboodles.'

'Toad-in-the-hole!' Blotto let out a low, shocked whistle. 'You really are up a gumtree without your teeth, Dippy! If it's not religion that gives the gel such bizarre notions, then what is it? Is there a history of insanity in the family? Because there are some very brainy bonkers-doctors around these days, who might be able to—'

'No, there's nothing squiffy about Poppy's sanity. She just says that our love is so pure, that it doesn't need any artificial stimulants to preserve it.'

'What, not even a half-bott of the club claret?'

'Not even a small sherry at Christmas.'

Blotto was beginning to see the extent of his old muffin-toaster's predicament. He knew that women had an irrational tendency to bring love into all of their dealings, but to use love to deny a boddo the human right of drinking . . . Well, that was way outside the rule book.

Still, he was with a chum, and he knew that the thing to do with chums was to dig them out of the mope-marshes. If he wasn't allowed to facilitate that process with drink, then he'd do it with food. 'Come on, Dippy!' he said. 'We're going straight to the dining room, where I am going to spoffing well buy you lunch. Won't be up to Xavier's standards, I'm afraid, but the Gren can still do a decent—'

'No, Blotters, it can't be done.'

'What on earth are you cluntering on about?'

'Poppy doesn't like me eating away from home.'

'Well, I suppose I can understand, if you've got Xavier's expertise to call on, then—'

'Poppy's sacked Xavier.'

'*What?*' It took a moment before the winded Blotto recouped enough breath to add, '*Why?*'

'Poppy says that feeding someone is one of the greatest expressions of human love . . .'

'Yes, I'd buy that in a bargain basement, but—'

'. . . and she says that our love is so pure that she is going to express hers for me by seeing to it that she cooks every meal for me.'

'Well, I'll be snickered . . . But, Dippy, Dippy old man . . . Is Poppy as good a cook as Xavier?'

Blotto saw loyalty fight with truth in his friend's face, and saved him the anguish of answering, by asking another question. 'To put it at its most basic level, Dippy me old shrimping net . . . Can Poppy cook?'

Again, there was no reply, but the way Dippy Le Froom's hand went instinctively to rub his stomach in anticipation of indigestions to come, gave a more potent answer than words could ever have done.

'So, Dippy, not to shimmy round the shrubbery, given the gluepot you're in: if you're not drinking and you're not eating, why on earth have you come here today?'

A tear glinted in his friend's eye. 'I've come to say goodbye,' he said.

'Goodbye? Goodbye to the Gren?'

'Yes, Blotters,' came the mournful reply.

'But why? No one ever leaves the Gren . . . unless they're drummed out for thimble-rigging. Why on earth are you leaving, Dippy?'

'Poppy says I no longer need to be a member of the Gren . . . not now I've got *her*.'

The Blotto who sat down at a table on his own in the Gren's dining room was a sober one. (That is, of course, not to say that he hadn't been sluicing his tonsils with the cream of the club's wine list. It was his mood that was sober.)

His encounter with Dippy Le Froom had shifted the barometer of his moods to 'changeable'. It had confirmed Blotto's every prejudice against the institution of marriage. And yet that was the stable into which the Dowager Duchess was inexorably leading him. His fate would be decided by the Hunt Ball at the end of the month. And the agent who destroyed all his boyish hopes and dreams would be Araminta fffrench-Wyndeau (with two silent *f*s). The die was cast.

'Blotto, you poor thimble,' demanded a cheery voice.

'What's put lumps in your custard? Lunching in the Gren on your own? That's not your usual size of pyjama.'

Blotto looked up from his thin soup to greet another of his Old Etonian muffin-toasters. In colour, Giles 'Whiffler' Tortington's face bore more than a passing resemblance to a rare sirloin. And the buttons of his tweed waistcoat fought a losing battle with his increasing girth. 'May I join you for lunch, Blotters?'

'On one condition.'

Puzzlement spread across Whiffler's honest features. 'Conditions? What's this?'

'Promise me that you'll be drinking.'

'Me? Drinking?' said Whiffler, as he speedily took his seat. 'Is the King German?'

Blotto had had a couple of large brandy and sodas in the Marlborough Bar, and now noticed that he seemed to have got through a bottle of claret at the table. He waved to a waiter for another one.

Giles 'Whiffler' Tortington, obviously, like Blotto and Dippy Le Froom, had aristocratic connections. He was, in fact, son and heir to the Earl of Hartlepool. His mother, the Countess, had died many years back and, though his father was enjoying a healthy and disgraceful old age, the moment must inevitably come when his son Giles would inherit the title. Most young men would find this a delightful prospect, but not Whiffler. His ambitions, from schooldays onwards, had always been modest. All he wanted to do with his life was play cricket, drink in the Gren, and be a Stage-Door Johnny. The thought of giving up these harmless pastimes when he took on the responsibilities of Earldom was his secret sorrow, a burden he carried around with him, but of which he never spoke to his Old Etonian chums. The kinds of things one talked about with one's muffin-toasters were facts. Feelings were way beyond the barbed wire.

The waiter brought the second bottle of the club claret, and soon both lunchers had their glasses charged.

'So, what's the toast, Whiffler?'

'Health and happiness!' came the uncontroversial response.

'And death to marriage!' added Blotto. They toasted each other accordingly. 'No, we're bong on the nose there, Whiffler. Only way a boddo can get on with his life is by keeping women out of it.'

'I wouldn't say that, Blotters.'

'What?' Blotto looked puzzled. He hadn't anticipated argument on the subject. Ever since he'd known Whiffler, they'd agreed on everything (except for one minor difference of opinion in their early teens about how close to the batsman a silly mid-off should be placed on a cricket field). Blotto had certainly not expected any argument from his friend on the matter of the fair sex.

'Women can be rather wonderful,' said Whiffler, in the dazed manner of someone who'd just been hit over the head with a stone-filled sock.

'Come on, you can't mean that. You're jiggling my kneecap, aren't you?'

'Never more serious in my life, Blotters. Of course, I'm not saying *all* women are wonderful. But one is.'

'Don't talk such toffee.'

'I'm not talking toffee, Blotters. The truth of the matter is . . . I'm in love.'

'Oh,' said Blotto with the deepest sympathy, 'I *am* sorry.'

'Don't be sorry. It's the most wonderful thing to have happened to me since I scored that century in the Eton and Harrow match.'

Blotto tried to lift himself out of the low mood engendered by his encounter with Dippy Le Froom. 'Well, it may not last,' he reassured Whiffler.

'Oh, but it will. Frou-Frou and I are for ever.'

'I beg your pardon, Whiffler me old sauce boat, but did my lugs deceive me, or did you say "Frou-Frou"?'

'Nothing wrong with your lugs, Blotters. They're

16

factory-fresh. I did say "Frou-Frou". And I was referring to the most beautiful girl in the world, Frou-Frou Gavotte.'

'Spoffing odd name. Is she foreign?'

'No, as English as a ham sandwich with mustard. She's an actress.'

'Oh?' said Blotto with huge relief. 'That's all right then.' His worries about Whiffler's future were at an end. Like bishops, over the years many Old Etonians had had a great deal of fun with actresses, but none of them would have gone as far as marrying one. Blotto raised his glass of claret in salutation. 'Top of the foxtail to you, me old fly-button! I've been shinnying up the wrong drainpipe. I thought you were going to tell me you were thinking of marrying this Frou-Frou.'

'But I am,' Whiffler protested.

'She's an actress.'

'Yes, one of the finest and most talented actresses currently to be seen on the London stage.'

'I'm sure she's an absolute eyewobbler too. But the fact remains that she's an actress. I can't see your Aged Parent welcoming one of those into the ancestral purlieus.'

'I don't care what the Aged P says. He can cut me off with a brass button if he wants to. Never mind the Pater: Genghis Khan and his Mongol Hordes couldn't stop me from marrying Frou-Frou!'

Blotto considered raising the possibility that Genghis Khan and his Mongol Hordes might have other priorities, but he remained silent. Though Blotto was normally a fluent fat-chewer, Whiffler's announcement had momentarily robbed him of the power of speech. He had actually met his friend's Aged P, the Earl of Hartlepool. As well as a good few acres in Central London, the noble peer owned most of Shropshire and sizeable chunks of adjacent counties. His likely response to his son and heir marrying an actress could, by Blotto's reckoning, cause an eruption comparable to that of Krakatoa. But it wasn't the moment to point that out.

'You must see Frou-Frou,' urged his friend. 'Then you'll agree with me that she is the most beautiful woman in the world.'

Nor was it the moment for Blotto to point out that that particular berth was already occupied by his sister, so he just said, 'I'm sure I'd be delighted to make her acquaintance at some point.'

'What about tonight?'

'Tonight?'

'Come on, you're in London. Have you got other plans for this evening?'

'Well, I was lining up for nosebags at the Savoy with my sister Twinks.'

'Bring her along. We can have dinner after the show.'

'What show is this?'

'*Light and Frothy.* It's the new intimate revue at the Pocket Theatre. Frou-Frou's the star. You'll love it, Blotters. Go on, say you'll come!'

'Tickey-Tockey,' said Blotto.

Light and Frothy

'When the news looks bad
And the people sad
And the clothes on your back are mothy . . .
When your spirits droop,
There's a fly in your soup
And a cockroach in your coffee . . .
When the future's dark
And you've lost your spark
And you cannot smile for toffee . . .
Well, a wise man said:
You must clear your head
And keep it Light and Frothy.'

While the chorus of white-clad flappers oo-ooed in the background, Frou-Frou Gavotte and her male partner, the immaculately suited Jack Carmichael, broke into a burst of manic tap-dancing. It ended with them forming a mirror image, conjoined by one hand and stretching the other out as far away as they could. Then, to applause filling the Pocket Theatre, they coiled back towards each other till they were arm in arm. The showgirls behind them stilled, as the pair of them sang the final chorus:

'Light and Frothy . . .

That's what the wise man said.
Light and Frothy . . .
Now your cares have fled.
Light and Frothy . . .
That must be your mood.
Light and Frothy . . .
That's the attitude.
As you face each day,
Cast your cares away,
Shout "Hip-hip-hooray!"
And make sure you stay . . .
Light . . . and . . . Frothy!'

The pair held their pose to wild applause, as the curtain fell. The sound redoubled as it rose again. First the chorus girls danced forward to acknowledge their part of the ovation. Then the supporting featured players took their bows. Finally, from the wings on either side, Frou-Frou Gavotte and Jack Carmichael entered. They joined hands. A deep bow and curtsey were granted to the ecstatic audience, who rose to their feet in acclamation.

Though very few of the people in the tiny Pocket Theatre could remember all the sketches and songs they had just witnessed, all of them felt that they'd had a really good time. That was certainly true of the party in the box that Giles 'Whiffler' Tortington had organised. Only Twinks had been slightly disappointed by the false rhymes in some of the lyrics. So far as she was concerned, 'coffee' and 'toffee' could never rhyme with 'frothy'. And she immediately distrusted any writer who thought he could get away with that kind of laziness. But then she always had been a stickler when it came to respect for the English language.

The writing of *Light and Frothy*'s sketches hadn't impressed her much more than the lyrics. For her, the humour of the show had fallen just the wrong side of whimsical.

20

But she had admired the style of the costumes. It was with no surprise she read in the programme that they'd all been creations of her own favourite couturier, Madame Clothilde of Mayfair.

Reservations about the writing aside, she had enjoyed the evening. And, despite being a past mistress at the art of discouraging the attentions of men, Twinks could not help acknowledging that Jack Carmichael was exceptionally good-looking.

Whiffler, of course, had made no secret of his adoration for Frou-Frou Gavotte. Every moment she was onstage, his eyes looked as if they were about to pop out on to his shirt front.

Blotto, too, found something in *Light and Frothy* that tickled his fancy. There was a girl in the sketches who played the cheeky, soubrette roles. She rejoiced in the name of Dolly Diller and spoke in a throaty Cockney voice, which had a very powerful effect on Blotto's sensibilities. Her black, bob-cut hair reminded him of a former love, the film star Mimsy La Pim. But Mimsy had suffered from many disadvantages, not least among them being American, while Dolly was as English as jellied eels. Blotto, with the ill-defined optimism which characterised all of his relations with women, wondered whether he might get an opportunity to meet her after the show.

Neither he, nor Twinks, nor Whiffler, had been aware of the man who slipped into the back of the theatre near the end of the revue, and trained a revolver on their box. But for the standing ovation, which blocked his sightline, he would have pulled the trigger.

'God, you look ravishing,' said Jack Carmichael.

'Oh, don't talk such toffee,' came Twinks's instinctive response. But she couldn't deny that the man had piqued her interest. Close to, he looked even better than he had from the auditorium. He was as lithe and toned as a panther. He'd undone his white tie, and a white towel hung around his neck. Over his make-up there was a sheen of sweat from his exertions in the dancing.

Twinks recognised the glazed look in his eyes. In common with so many amorous swains before, Jack Carmichael had fallen for her like a guardsman in a heatwave. But in his case, she didn't mind. When he suggested they go out for dinner together, she thought the idea was 'Splendissimo!'

In the adjacent dressing room, Giles 'Whiffler' Tortington sported the same glazed expression as Jack Carmichael had. But his was directed towards Frou-Frou Gavotte, whose stage costume had now been replaced by a peignoir as light and frothy as the show she had just completed.

In Blotto's view, she was a pretty enough girl, though Twinks obviously had the edge in the Most Beautiful Girl in the World Competition. His sister, he knew, would have romped it against any opposition.

Frou-Frou Gavotte could have been described as blonde and petite, both of which adjectives matched her French name. Her voice, however, when not using the clipped vowels required on stage, was pure, rasping Cockney. Because of his somewhat sheltered background, Blotto had not had the good fortune to meet a Billingsgate fishwife, but, if he had, then he would have known that Frou-Frou sounded exactly like one.

It seemed unlikely that Whiffler's Aged P had ever met a Billingsgate fishwife either (you don't see many of those round Hunt Balls – or the House of Lords, come to that), but Blotto was still not certain that he would warm to one as a prospective daughter-in-law. Whiffler himself was blind to any kind of objections that might be made. He was, of course, looking with the eyes of love.

'Isn't Frou-Frou just wonderful in the show?' he demanded of his friend.

'Oh, a real cork-popper,' Blotto agreed loyally. 'And some of the song lyrics were definitely out of the top layer of the chocolate box.'

'They were all right, but it's the performance that turns them into pure creamy éclair,' said Whiffler dismissively.

'What's the name of the boddo who writes the lyrics, Frou-Frou?' asked Blotto.

'Everard Stoop,' she replied. 'He writes the sketches too. He's frightfully clever.'

'Vastly overrated,' said Whiffler, unwilling to hear any other man praised by his beloved.

Frou-Frou looked set to argue with this assertion, but their conversation was interrupted by the explosion into the room of the small bundle of energy that was Dolly Diller. She was out of her *Light and Frothy* costume, and into a pink silk dress that stopped vertiginously high above her white-stockinged knees. Blotto looked as though Christmas, his birthday and a massive win on a rank outsider in the Grand National had all happened on the same day.

''Ello, darlin'!' screamed Dolly.

''Ello, darlin'!' screamed Frou-Frou. 'You know Whiffler, dontcha?'

'Course I do.' She slapped a darker red lipstick imprint on the red Old Etonian face. 'You're always coming back like a bad oyster, aintcher, Whiffles?'

'And this is his friend ... What did you say he was called?'

'Devereux Lyminster, Frou-Frou. Younger brother of the Duke of Tawcester.'

'Yes, but everyone calls me "Blotto".'

'Blotto? That's a nice name,' said Dolly, in a throaty voice which, had Blotto known the word, he would have recognised as 'sexy'. 'And fancy you being the brother of a Duke, and all.'

He offered his hand. He'd rather have been offering his

cheek to receive a smacker like the one Whiffler had got, but recognised that he didn't yet know Dolly that well. She took the outstretched hand in both of hers, though, and shook it with encouraging warmth. He got the feeling she was a very warm person.

'Nice name for a nice boy, eh?' she susurrated. 'You're a looker, and no mistake, aintcher?'

'Oh. Well. Thank you.' Compliments always made Blotto feel rather embarrassed. Boldly, he ventured the opinion that: 'You're a bit of a bellbuzzer yourself, Dolly.'

'Well, thank you, kind sir.' She dropped a mock curtsey.

'In fact,' Blotto continued, with even greater daring, 'you're a real bellbuzzer with three veg and gravy.'

'Ooh, you flatterer, you!'

Blotto gaped at her, jaw sagging. Rarely had he been so quick in expressing his attraction for a woman. And the hasty effort had left his word-hoard severely depleted. He continued to gape.

Then Giles 'Whiffler' Tortington had one of his rare but magnificent inspirations. 'Great galumphing goatherds!' he said. 'Blotters and I were going to take Frou-Frou out for a scrimmick of dinner. Why don't you join us, Dolly?'

Blotto looked gratefully across at his friend. Old Etonians could always rely on their muffin-toasters. They were the sort of boddoes with whom one would voluntarily go into the jungle, a Hunt Ball, or any other dangerous environment. Blotto didn't think he'd been so grateful since Whiffler had claimed responsibility for writing 'Old Blaggers Eats Snails!' on their French master's blackboard (even though anyone could have recognised that the words were in Blotto's handwriting). Among the right sort of people, *noblesse* still did very definitely *oblige*.

'Ooh, wouldn't I just love that?' Dolly Diller gurgled.

'Well, come on, Frou-Frou,' said Whiffler. 'Get out of the old peignoir and into some suitably totty togs, and we'll be on our way!'

* * *

24

Dolly Diller stayed in the dressing room while her friend changed, but Blotto and Whiffler, who had, after all, been to public school and knew their etiquette, waited in the corridor outside.

They had only been there a couple of minutes, when Twinks flashed by on the arm of the ravishing Jack Carmichael. 'Going out for dinner, Blotto me old herring-gutter,' she called over her shoulder. 'See you at the Savvers in the morning!'

'Tickey-Tockey,' said her brother.

He and Whiffler might have said more, had not a small man in a black suit, black shirt, black beret (and no tie!) at that moment walked past them, as if about to enter the dressing room. Whiffler interposed himself between man and door.

'Excuse me, old greengage,' he said, 'but Frou-Frou Gavotte's changing her togs in there.'

'So?' demanded the newcomer, in a voice that marked him out as that most unappealing of specimens, a Frenchman. 'Girls' bodies hold no surprises for me. Particularly the bodies of these particular girls. You see, I *own* every woman in *Light and Frothy*. They are all mine.'

This was a bit much for Whiffler. 'They are spoffing well not yours! At least, Frou-Frou certainly isn't! And if you dare to claim that she is again, then I will ask you to step outside to settle the matter.'

'Poo,' said the man, in the way that only a Frenchman can say 'Poo'. 'How very English – you think you can settle every dispute with a fight.'

'Well, that approach didn't turn out too shabbily for us at Agincourt,' asserted Blotto.

This prompted another 'Poo' from the Frenchman. 'You clearly do not know who I am.'

'I know,' said Whiffler, 'that you are an oikish louse with no respect for the fair sex – and, quite frankly, that's all I need to know!'

The Frenchman drew himself up to his full height, at which he almost reached Blotto and Whiffler's second shirt studs. 'My name is Pierre Labouze . . . the internationally known impresario. *Light and Frothy* is my latest creation. I have devised and put together the whole show. *Light and Frothy* is a Pierre Labouze production. So, when I say that I own all of the women in *Light and Frothy*, I am speaking no more than the truth.'

'Listen, *monsieur*—' began Whiffler, the rest of his face now redder than the lipstick mark Dolly Diller had placed on it.

'No, you listen! I am not willing to be insulted in my own theatre by a . . .' He paused to gather enough venom for the insult '. . . by a *Stage-Door Johnny*!'

'I am not a Stage-Door Johnny,' Whiffler responded with some dignity. 'I am a Stage-Door Giles.'

'I do not care. Whatever your name, you are an irrelevance!'

Blotto had had enough. 'Are you calling my friend an "irrelevance"?'

'Yes,' Pierre Labouze confirmed in a combative tone.

'Well, I must ask you not to,' said Blotto.

'Why?'

'Because I don't know what it means,' he admitted.

The argument might have progressed further, had not the dressing-room door at that point opened to reveal Frou-Frou Gavotte, now dressed in her evening finery, with Dolly Diller just behind her. The jaws of Whiffler and Blotto dropped in unison at their combined pulchritude.

But their boss, the creator of *Light and Frothy*, was less than impressed. 'Frou-Frou, you missed the beat in your Toe Tap Buck Break in "How Do You Get a Plumber in the Summer?" And, Dolly, in "Seaside Serenade", you were slow on the cue. After Jack's line, "I just seem to have lost my zing", if you do not come in quickly with, "I just seem to have found mine", the joke is lost. It did not even get a laugh tonight.'

26

'It never gets a bloomin' laugh,' the soubrette came back combatively, 'and that's because it's not a funny line.'

'But it was written by Everard Stoop,' Pierre Labouze protested, 'and Everard Stoop is acknowledged to be the wittiest man in London.'

'Yeah?' said Dolly Diller. 'I've heard wittier lines than his down a boozer in the Balls Pond Road.'

'You cannot say that about Everard Stoop!'

'I've just said it, so you can put that in your pipe and smoke it . . . Boozy.'

'And I have told you a million times not to call me "Boozy"!'

'Well, that's a million and one now, isn't it, Boozy? Oops, a million and two.'

Blotto was greatly enjoying this exchange. He wasn't quite sure, but he thought he probably liked a girl with spirit.

'Dolly,' snarled the impresario, 'you are just a common slut!'

'Now rein in the roans a moment there,' said Blotto. 'Don't forget you're talking to a lady.'

'Lady? If that's a lady, I'm a Dutchman.'

'Well, you're not a Dutchman,' asserted Blotto, 'but you still suffer the appalling disadvantage of not being British. You're a Frenchman, which is an even worse kind of stencher.'

'How dare you speak of my countrymen like that!' His Gallic temperament flared. 'You are speaking of the country of Napoleon.'

'Tickey-Tockey,' Blotto agreed. 'But we're speaking *in* the country of Wellington. And we all know how that particular ding-dong turned out, don't we?'

This caught the impresario on the raw. 'Are you looking for a horsewhipping, monsieur?'

'Why?' asked Blotto, looming over his potential combatant. 'Are you proposing to deliver one?'

'Not. No personally. But I know people who could flay you to within a centimetre of your life.'

Blotto looked confused. The Eton curriculum hadn't covered the metric system.

Frou-Frou and Dolly took advantage of the silence to say they thought they were meant to be going out to dinner.

'Not until you have done what I demand of you!' screamed Pierre Labouze. 'I demand that you both come back onstage with me immediately, so that we can rehearse those moments in the show which tonight failed to come up to my high standards!'

'And I demand,' said Frou-Frou, with implacable Cockney determination, 'that you stop getting your smalls in a spiral, and get out the way! We're going out for dinner. See you in time for the show tomorrow.'

With that, she and Dolly swept past the spluttering impresario, with two even more admiring swains in their wake. Blotto did not even bother to make a face at his vanquished opponent.

Like a spoilt child – or like a Frenchman, which comes to much the same thing – Pierre Labouze stamped his little foot.

The crowd of departing audience had thinned by the time they got to the front of the Pocket Theatre. Jack Carmichael had already whisked Twinks away in his Hispano-Suiza, and Corky Froggett was sitting patiently in the Lagonda, ready to spirit Blotto off in whatever direction he chose. Corky would have been equally happy, whether the destination proved to be the dry veldt of Africa, the snows of the Himalayas or the mountains of Peru. And if the journey took them into a warzone, where the opportunity arose for the chauffeur to kill a few people before laying down his life for the young master, then he would be even happier.

There was one other car waiting in front of the Pocket

Theatre, a black saloon with tinted windows. Beside it stood two men in black overcoats, with black hats pulled down over their eyes. Before Blotto had even had the opportunity to suggest they should all travel to their dinner destination in the Lagonda, the two men stepped forward, grabbed hold of Giles 'Whiffler' Tortington and bundled him into the back of the car.

By the time Blotto had recovered from the shock of this sudden action, Whiffler and his abductors had disappeared into the dark streets of London.

4

Stratagems at the Savvers

'So, what happened to you last night, Twinks me old button-hook?'

'I had a very pleasant dinner, thank you, Blotto me old soup-strainer.'

'With that hoofer boddo, Jim McMickle?'

'Jack Carmichael, yes.'

'And what time did you get back here to the Savvers?'

Blotto felt a rare jolt of disapproval from his sister's azure eyes. 'Really, Blotters? You sound just like the Mater.'

'Ouch! You know how to hurt a chap.'

'Well, stop twitching your nostrils about what time I wheeled out the jim-jams.'

'Sorry, sis.'

'So you should be.'

Blotto had been down to breakfast in the Savoy dining room before Twinks. When he'd taken his seat, he'd been manically desperate to tell her about the events of the previous evening, but the profusion of bacon, egg, sausages, kidneys, kippers, kedgeree and other delights in the silver dishes had distracted him. Though long on such sterling qualities as bravery, loyalty and honour, Blotto had always been a bit short on attention span.

And it was only some time after Twinks had arrived and asked, 'Did you have a splendiferous evening with the delectable Miss Diller?' that he remembered he had a story to tell.

By the end of his narration, all of the bacon, egg, sausages, kidneys, kippers, kedgeree and other delights on his plates had gone cold.

'So, Blotto, you didn't get your dinner *à deux* with Dolly?'

'No. Though, mind you, it was never intended to be a dinner *à deux*. It was going to be a dinner *à . . . à . . . à . . .*' He wished he'd listened more during his French lessons at Eton. 'Dinner *à four*,' he concluded feebly.

'But, whatever it was going to be, you didn't get to eat it?'

'No. Apart from anything else, Frou-Frou was in absolute crimps about what had happened to Whiffler. Anyway, by the time the police had finished questioning us—'

'Oh, don't tell me you brought in the flatties!' Twinks's beautiful face wore a pale mask of disappointment. 'I thought we had a sign-on-the-dotted about this, Blotters. We only bring in the bizz-bods when we've solved the case. Bringing them in early really is the flea's armpit.'

'I didn't bring the stenchers in,' Blotto protested. 'It was the theatre manager. He'd pinged the telephonic instrument before I had a chance to stop him.'

'Oh well,' said Twinks, 'let's turn the cloud round and see the silver. If the flatties are already involved, then our challenge is to see that we nail the perps before they do. Which, of course we will do, as easy as raspberries.'

Blotto looked dubious. For a moment, his internal barometer wavered towards 'Changeable'. 'Hold the hounds for a moment there, sis. I know back home we can wriggle rings around the local constabulary. Chief Inspector Trumbull and Sergeant Knatchbull are the world's worst voidbrains.' (Which some authorities might have considered a bit rich, given who was speaking.) 'But here in London, we're up against the cream of Scotland

Yard. We haven't got a candle's chance in a cloudburst against them.'

'Oh, Blotto, don't talk such meringue. The cream of Scotland Yard are all clotted. We've got the brains to run them rippy.'

'I think, actually, Twinks,' said her brother with modest, but accurate, self-estimation, *'you'*ve got the brains to run them rippy.'

'Don't nit-pick noodles! We're a team. We're going to find out what's happened to Whiffler, we're going to rescue him. And, what's more, we're going to do it before the cream of Scotland Yard have finished tying up their bootlaces!'

'Oh, Twinks,' said Blotto, once again full of admiration. 'You really are the panda's panties.' Then he added eagerly, 'How are we going to do it?'

'Well,' said his sister, 'I might have to have a little cogitette about that. I'll go up to my suite and rustle up a plan of action.' She rose from her chair, causing a flurry of high blood pressure amongst the many married men in the dining room, who weren't used to seeing such pulchritude at the breakfast table.

'But, Twinks me old Ouija board,' said an appalled Blotto, 'you haven't had anything to eat.'

'I'll order Room Service,' said his sister. 'Meet me for a starcher in the American Bar at twelve-thirty.' And she glided out, trailed by the hungry looks of all those married men.

Now Twinks was on the case, Blotto felt secure. His barometer was once again set fair. He gestured to a waiter to bring him another plate, which he proceeded to fill up with more bacon, egg, sausages, kidneys, kippers, kedgeree and other delights.

'I've spoken to Frou-Frou Gavotte,' Twinks announced.

'What? How did you get her telephone number?'

'Easy as a housemaid's virtue. I rang the Pocket Theatre. And the result is that Frou-Frou is joining us for lunch.'

They were standing at the American Bar, watching the creation of their pre-luncheon cocktails. From the extensive list available, Twinks had, by coincidence, ordered a Housemaid's Virtue. Blotto had opted for his favourite, St Louis Steamhammer. The barman's dexterity was as much part of the entertainment as the jazz piano tinkling away in the background.

'I say, Twinks me old pan-scourer, you didn't think to ask Dolly Diller too, did you?'

'Why in the name of strawberries would I do that?'

'Oh. No spoffing reason,' said Blotto. But he couldn't suppress a slight disappointment.

'I've invited Frou-Frou Gavotte because she's apparently got the wiggles for "Whiffler" Tortington. So, she might have some idea who the stenchers are who kidnapped him . . .'

'Good ticket,' said Blotto.

'. . . whereas I am unaware of any connection between Dolly Diller and Whiffler.'

'Tickey-Tockey,' said Blotto. It was always wise to agree when his sister started to sound like their mother.

The cocktails were handed across by the barman, his antennae finely tuned to their first reactions. Twinks took a sip from her Housemaid's Virtue and felt its beneficence tingle through every capillary to the furthest point of her nerve endings. Blotto took a substantial slug from his St Louis Steamhammer, and waited for the familiar sensation of being poleaxed by a poleaxe.

The barman smiled with the satisfaction of a job well done.

'When a man is tired of London, he might as well move to the country.'

The words, spoken in a light, clipped voice, were greeted

33

by a ripple of appreciative giggles. Blotto and Twinks looked across to the speaker. Though it was lunchtime, he wore a red velvet smoking jacket with black silk lapels. The skin on his face was very dry and tight, as though he might have spent time in tropical climes. One hand held a Martini, and the other a tortoiseshell cigarette holder of inordinate length. He was surrounded by a coterie of young men, who were the ones supplying giggles to his aphorisms.

'London,' he continued, 'not Oxford, is the city of dreaming spires. Some dream of it, some aspire to it.' Once again, the acolytes giggled.

'If London didn't exist, it would be necessary to invent it.' Cue for more hilarity.

'Who is that self-aggrandising excrescence?' Twinks hissed to the barman.

'Ooh, I'm surprised you don't recognise him, Madam. He's Everard Stoop.'

'That's the boddo who wrote *Light and Frothy*,' said Blotto.

'He's the wittiest man in London,' the barman asserted.

'That doesn't say much for the other wits in London,' observed Twinks, in full Dowager Duchess mode.

As if to prove her point, Everard Stoop announced, 'Every inch in London is better than a mile in the countryside.' At this sally, his covey of young men had difficulty in containing their mirth.

Blotto and Twinks turned away, to find a table out of earshot of these blunted shafts of wit, but were stopped when they heard Everard Stoop say, 'Ah, but who is this? A thing of beauty is a beautiful thing.'

They turned back to see Everard kissing Frou-Frou Gavotte on both cheeks, in the excessive Continental manner. The revue star had clearly just arrived in the American Bar, and had not yet seen her luncheon hosts.

'Good to see you, Everard old cock.'

'And you too, Frou-Frou. You know, of course, that I

adore you frou and frou.' The giggles of the young men rose to an even higher pitch.

'And tell me, darling, how did my wonderful little show at the Pocket Theatre go last night?'

'Oh, lummee, Everard. Haven't you heard?'

'No, I've never been one to follow the *heard instinct*.' He thought that particular one was so funny, he even allowed himself a little laugh at it. And the young men giggled helplessly.

'Ooh, it was terrible. I'm still bent out of shape about it.' But, before Frou-Frou launched into her narrative, she noticed Blotto and Twinks. 'Oh, hi!' she shrieked out across the bar. 'I don't think you've met Everard Stoop.'

Introductions were duly made. Because she had gone straight to Jack Carmichael's dressing room, Twinks hadn't met Frou-Frou the night before.

'And have you seen *Light and Frothy*?' asked its writer, eager for praise (like all writers). 'It is absolutely the hottest ticket in town.'

'Oh yes, went last night,' said Blotto. 'Beezer show.'

'It had its moments,' said Twinks coolly.

'Not only moments,' Everard Stoop quipped back. 'It also had *momentum*.'

The young men roared, as the writer narrowed his small eyes and took in Twinks. 'I say, you're a bit of a bobby-dazzler, aren't you?'

'Don't talk such meringue.'

'Beauty,' Everard Stoop pronounced, 'is in the eye of the cigarette holder.'

While his coterie held each other's sides in merriment, Twinks said drily, 'I think it's time we went through for lunch.'

'I'm really frightened about what might have happened to him,' said Frou-Frou. 'There are some nasty types in

London. I just hate the idea of Whiffler getting hurt. I'm worried sick.'

Being worried sick, Blotto and Twinks observed, had not had any effect on Frou-Frou's appetite. She was wolfing down roast beef and all the trimmings like there was no tomorrow. (They didn't know that actors always wolf food down like there's no tomorrow. However successful they end up, they never forget the days when they didn't know where the next meal was coming from.)

'May I ask,' said Twinks, 'how long you and Whiffler had been . . . er, sharing the same umbrella?'

'Ooh, he was at the First Night of *Light and Frothy*. Come round afterwards he did. Said he'd got the hotties for my totties. Asked me to go out for dinner with him that night. But I . . . um . . .' She coloured. 'I wasn't free that night. Next evening, though, he was there again. He said he was turning up like a bad penny. I said he was turning up like a *good* penny. He doesn't realise, you see, Whiffler doesn't, what a gorgeous man he is.' She turned the beam of her eyes on Blotto. 'You've known him for a long time. You think he's a gorgeous man, don't you?'

Blotto's face turned almost as red as that of his missing friend. Boddoes who'd been muffin-toasters together at Eton didn't notice what other boddoes looked like. Wasn't polite. They'd certainly never describe each other as 'gorgeous'. Confused, Blotto responded that Whiffler had always been a 'Grade A foundation stone'.

'And gorgeous too,' Frou-Frou insisted.

'Thoroughly decent cove, by any measure of tape,' Blotto agreed. And assuming that his friend had inducted his inamorata into the mysteries of cricket, he added, 'And a very steady Number Four in the batting order.'

Frou-Frou made no comment, but continued, 'So, we went out for dinner after the second night of the show. And that was it, really. We been . . . sharing the same umbrella ever since.'

'And how long ago is that?' asked Twinks. 'How long has *Light and Frothy* been running?'

'Nearly three months,' replied Frou-Frou, as if in awe, not of the show's, but of the liaison's longevity.

'And, during that time, did Whiffler ever suggest to you that he might have any enemies?'

'Only his father,' replied Frou-Frou.

Twinks nodded. Like her brother, she knew the Earl of Hartlepool. She didn't need any explanation of his inevitable Krakatoa-scale reaction to a marriage between his heir and the star of *Light and Frothy*. Frou-Frou just wasn't Countess material.

'Yes, but why would they kidnap him?' Twinks asked.

'To take him back to their castle or whatever-it-is in Shropshire and force him to marry some simpering pea-brain who comes from the right kind of family.'

Twinks was about to reply haughtily that that was not how the English aristocracy behaved, but when she stopped to think about it, she realised that was *exactly* how the English aristocracy had always behaved. Their history was littered with examples of abductions and forced marriages. But such behaviour still seemed out of character for the Earl of Hartlepool. He was not a man to achieve his ends by force. In fact, Twinks recalled, the old boy was deeply involved in some organisation that campaigned for a total ban on firearms.

'Let's change tack for a moment here, Frou-Frou,' she said. Have *you* got any enemies?'

'Enemies?'

'Yes, you know,' Blotto chipped in. 'Four-faced filchers who'll sell you up the river for a handful of winkle shells.'

'Oh, I don't think I know anyone like that,' said Frou-Frou Gavotte demurely.

'What about in the theatre business?' suggested Twinks. 'I've heard it said that it's hard to get to the top without trampling on a few fingers.'

'I've always got on like a house on fire with everyone I've worked with.' Still very demure.

'What about that Boozy boddo who came to your dressing room last night?' asked Blotto. 'He was a stencher if ever I saw one. And French. And he had the brass front to claim that he owned you. Not only that he owned you, but that he owned Dolly as well.'

'Pierre Labouze is just like that: all mouth and no trousers.'

'He had trousers on last night,' said Blotto, pleased at having caught her out in an inexactitude. 'Black trousers. Black shirt. No tie – that's always the mark of the oikish sponge-worm, but then what do you expect from the French?'

'Are you saying, Frou-Frou,' asked Twinks, 'that this Pierre Labouze, whoever he may be—'

'He's the producer of the show. The impresario.'

'And are you saying that he threatened you?'

'He spoffing well did,' said Blotto. 'I was there. I heard the stencher.'

'Like I said,' insisted Frou-Frou, 'Pierre is all talk. He wouldn't hurt a fly. He certainly wouldn't have hurt Whiffler. Apart from anything else, he was still inside the theatre when the abduction took place.'

'Well, I suppose that's all tiddle and pom,' said Twinks without enthusiasm. 'But if the crime wasn't committed by someone from your professional life, what about your private life then?'

'Starring in a West End revue, you don't have much time for a private life. Mine only really started when I met Whiffler.' Frou-Frou took a tiny handkerchief from her reticule and dabbed the corner of her eye with it. 'Oh, I wonder where the poor boy is right now.'

Twinks was not to be sidetracked by this show of emotion. 'Frou-Frou, could we get back in the box, please? Listen, you look absolutely splendiferous. You must be well into your thirt—'

'I was brought up to believe,' the actress interrupted, 'that ladies never talk about their age.'

'Unlike you, I happen to *be* a lady,' Twinks responded acerbically, 'and, in my experience, they talk about little else. Anyway, don't shuffle round the shrubbery, Frou-Frou. You know what I mean. You haven't got to your age ...' That prompted a small wince '... without other men having had the wiggles for you. Ex-lovers are always risky fish. Isn't it possible that one of them might have resented seeing Whiffler slipping into the favourite's saddle ... ?'

'I don't know what you mean.' When Frou-Frou Gavotte felt like playing the dumb blonde, she could play it very well.

'I can't be much plainer,' snapped Twinks. 'Do you think one of your ex-boyfriends might have abducted Whiffler?'

'Oh no. I don't think so.'

'Toad-in-the-hole! I've actually just had a buzzbanger of a thought!' said Blotto.

His sister looked across the table at him with some scepticism. Deeply though she loved her brother, she knew that his thoughts were not always in the first division. But she waited patiently while he expounded his idea.

'Chap I knew at Eton, Swiss boddo called Gunter Ehrlich – everyone called him "Holey".'

'Was he very religious?' asked Twinks.

'Great Wilberforce, no. It's just that, you know, Swiss cheese is full of holes.' Twinks did not comment on this fine example of schoolboy wit, as Blotto went on, 'Anyway, Holey's parents were as rich as Creosote.'

'I think you mean "Croesus",' suggested Twinks.

'Of course, they didn't get all the old jingle-jangle the proper way, you know, by inheriting it. They actually loaded up the loot by *working* for it.' The word was larded with contempt. 'Owned some big bank in Switzerland, I think. Anyway, they'd got the spondulicks dripping out their lugs. Everything they touched turned to gold, like that old pineapple, King Minus.'

'Midas,' Twinks suggested.

'Whoever. Anyway, Holey's Aged Ps apparently collected precious jewels – diamonds, rubies, emeralds. They had gemstones with every colour of the scrotum.'

'Spectrum,' suggested Twinks, who was beginning to wonder whether her brother would ever get to the point.

'So, without fiddling round the fir trees, what I'm saying is that they had plenty of the old golden gravy.'

'Yes, I think you've made that clear,' said his sister.

'Anyway, so it turned out that, one afternoon after cricket, we went back to the old boarding house for supper, and there was no sign of Holey. Not a single nostril hair. And do you know what had happened?' Blotto paused for dramatic effect.

'He'd been kidnapped by some criminal stenchers and held to ransom.'

Her brother looked at Twinks in amazement. 'How do you know that? Have I trundled out this tale before?'

'No. I just worked it out.'

'Toad-in-the-hole! That brainbox of yours should be put in the British Museum.'

'So, what you're suggesting, Blotters, is that Whiffler might have been kidnapped by people who won't let him go until a ransom's been paid?'

'That's about the size of it, yes.'

'Splendissimo,' said Twinks. As her brother's ideas went, this wasn't a bad one. In fact, of all the ones he'd ever put forward to her, this probably won the Victor Ludorum. 'Give that pony a rosette!'

Blotto smiled bashfully. Boddoes like him had never been any good at accepting compliments.

'The big Q is, though,' Twinks went on, 'who are the lumps of toadspawn who might have abducted Whiffler?'

'Ah,' Blotto confessed. 'When it comes to that, I'm a bit of an empty revolver.'

'It's a splendiferous idea, bro, but I think we'd better wait till a ransom note appears.'

'Tickey-Tockey. I'll ring Reception and ask if anything in that line's been delivered.'

'Erm, Blotters ... I think it's more likely that a ransom demand would be sent to Whiffler's father, the Earl, rather than to you.'

'Ah,' said Blotto. 'Good ticket.'

'I'll contact him to see if I can get the SP on that.'

Blotto and Twinks both looked at Frou-Frou Gavotte, whose face bore an expression of boredom. As an actress, she wasn't used to being away from the centre of a conversation for so long.

'Any other stirrings in your grey cells, Frou-Frou?' asked Twinks. A shake of the blonde head. 'Then let us summon the dessert trolley.'

In the lift up to their suites, Twinks turned her azure eyes on to her brother's. 'I'd bet a guinea to a groat she's lying.'

'Well, I'll be snickered,' he said.

'Frou-Frou Gavotte knows more than she's letting on.'

5

The Short Arm of the Law

As soon as Twinks had reached her suite, she sat down at the writing desk and drew a notebook out of her sequinned reticule. She began by writing notes on the interview with Frou-Frou Gavotte. From those she developed more lines of enquiry into the abduction of Giles 'Whiffler' Tortington.

As soon as Blotto had reached his suite, he lay down on the bed to catch a little shuteye before it would be time to start the evening with another of the American barman's St Louis Steamhammers.

It was only a few moments later that he was recalled from innocent oblivion by the jangling of the bedside telephone. An obsequious voice informed him that there was a police officer at Reception who wished to speak to him. Blotto asked that the man should be directed up to his suite.

He was crossing the landing on the way to fetch Twinks when the lift doors opened, and a small man in a black bowler hat and black overcoat emerged. 'Are you Mr Devereux Lyminster?' he asked.

Blotto could not deny that he was.

'I am Detective Inspector Craig Dewar, of Scotland Yard.'

'Beezer to see you. You're the flattie who wants to ask me some questions?'

'That is correct, sir. Though I would like to say I am not very happy with the word "flattie".'

'Oh, so sorry. Fully understand. My Mater gets vinegared off too when people use abbreviations. Should have said "flatfoot".'

'Well, actually, I'd prefer you didn't use either—'

'I'll just fetch my sister, and then we can do the old chitter-chatter in my suite.'

'Excuse me, sir. Why do you want to fetch your sister?'

'Oh, you must understand, when it comes to brainpower, I'm a pygmy and she's Goliath. Always like to have her around if I'm being asked questions. She can help me out with the gummy ones.'

'But did your sister actually witness the abduction of Mr Tortington at the Pocket Theatre last night?'

'No, she wasn't actually there. She'd already gone off to nosebags with some actor boddo.'

'In that case, Mr Lyminster sir, I don't think there is any necessity for her to be present at our interview.'

'Oh,' said Blotto, not a little put out. Still, he knew one shouldn't unnecessarily antagonise those who represented the majesty of British Law. 'Tickey-Tockey then, if you say so.'

'I do say so, sir.'

Back inside his suite, Blotto was struck by how very short his interrogator was. But he wasn't about to be prejudiced by that. Some of the most lucrative days Blotto had enjoyed at the races had been thanks to the efforts of very short people.

Having taken the proffered seat, Detective Inspector Craig Dewar drew out from his pocket a battered blue-covered notebook and the stub of a pencil. He opened a new page and licked the point of his pencil. (This is something frequently done by fictional policemen and fictional reporters. It is an action rarely seen in real life. Presumably real-life policemen and real-life reporters sensibly try to avoid lead poisoning.)

'Well, Mr Lyminster,' he began ponderously, 'as someone who has spent his entire career at Scotland Yard, I am a great believer in teamwork.'

'Oh, me too. You're bong on the nose there, Inspector. Out on the cricket field, it's not you who counts, it's all the other greengages.'

'Exactly right. So, Mr Lyminster, assuming that you and I have the same aim in mind – to find Mr Tortington – it is important that we work together.'

'Hoopee-doopie,' Blotto agreed.

'So, if you get any new information which may lead to our solving the case, I hope you will pass it on to me as soon as possible.'

'Good ticket.'

'But only tell it to me. I can't overemphasise the importance of secrecy in a case like this.'

'Don't don your worry-boots about that, Inspector. Everything under the dustbin lid, I understand.'

'Good.'

'Oh, just one thingette . . . When you say I shouldn't spill the haricots to anyone, does that include my sister?'

'A general rule in these affairs, Mr Lyminster, is that the fewer people who know the details, the better.'

'Point taken and digested. I'll be as tight as a limpet with lockjaw.' The idea of conducting an investigation independent of Twinks was not without its attraction. Though he had enormous love and respect for his sister, Blotto liked the idea of doing something off his own cricket bat (without remembering the previous occasions when such a course had proved disastrous).

'Very well, Mr Lyminster . . .' Detective Inspector Craig Dewar licked the tip of his pencil again in a businesslike manner. 'As a witness to the abduction of Mr Tortington yesterday evening, I am sure you have a lot to tell me.'

'Well, he was abducted,' said Blotto. 'In a black saloon. By two men.'

'Are you sure it was only two men?'

'I only spoffing well saw two men.'

'And did they get into the front of the car or the back?'

'The back.'

'And the car then drove off?'

'Bong on the nose, Inspector.'

'So, are you suggesting that one of the men you saw was driving the car from the back seat?'

'Erm . . .'

'Or maybe it was a driverless car?' The Inspector chuckled heartily. He was enjoying himself. 'Though it'll be a strange world when such a thing as a driverless car exists, won't it, Mr Lyminster?'

'It certainly will, by Denzil.'

'So how many abductors do you reckon Mr Tortington had?'

Understanding broke through at last, like the sun from behind storm clouds, and irradiated Blotto's honest face. 'Three!' he replied with pride.

'At *least* three,' Dewar corrected him.

'Toad-in-the-hole!' murmured Blotto, deeply impressed. 'You've got a brainbox and a half, haven't you, Inspector. How did you work that out?'

'Oh,' came the casual reply, 'just a matter of logic. When you've been in the detection game as long as I have, Mr Lyminster, you find these kinds of deductions come instinctively. Every mystery eventually gives up its secrets to the processes of logic and minute examination of the known facts. The deduction is in the detail.'

'Well, I'll be battered like a pudding!'

'So, bearing what I've just said in mind, Mr Lyminster, could you tell me, *in detail*, exactly what happened last night when you and your party left the Pocket Theatre?'

Blotto started out by repeating his previous answer verbatim, but the shrewdly targeted questions from Detective Inspector Craig Dewar prompted a lot of extra recollection. He was able to give a more exact description of the overcoats and hats worn by the abductors. He recalled the dark stubbly chins which were all he could see of their faces. He confirmed that neither of them spoke.

'And what about their victim, Mr Lyminster? Did Mr Tortington say anything?'

'Well, not words exactly.'

'Not words? Then what?'

'As I recall, he let out a kind of yelp.'

'A yelp, Mr Lyminster?'

'Yes, you know, like when you tread on a puppy.'

'I have to confess, Mr Lyminster, that I have never trodden on a puppy.'

'Haven't you?' Blotto was amazed. Clearly the Inspector must have been brought up in the city. No one brought up in the country could have reached his age without treading on a puppy. Though very few people – and they were the worst kind of stenchers – actually trod on puppies deliberately, treading on puppies by accident was just one of the hazards of country life.

'Don't let's worry, Mr Lyminster, about the precise kind of yelp Mr Tortington emitted. Incidentally . . .' The Inspector took a fountain pen out of his pocket and wrote a number on the hotel notepad. 'This will find me at Scotland Yard. Any time of the day or night. If you have any thoughts on the case, even the smallest idea, don't hesitate to contact me.'

'Good ticket. And if my sister has any thoughts, shall I give her this number to—'

'Your sister is not to be given that number!'

'Tickey-Tockey.'

'Now, Mr Lyminster, let's move on to *your* view of the crime.'

'My view of the crime?'

'Yes. Surely, having witnessed the abduction, some thoughts must have gone through your head as to why it might have happened.'

'Erm . . .'

'You must have asked yourself *why* your friend should be the victim of kidnapping.'

'I'm not really a whale on asking myself things,' Blotto confessed. 'Or asking other people things, when it comes to it.' But then, once again, the sun burst through the clouds. 'Ah, I see. You're asking me what kind of stencher I think might have kidnapped old Whiffler.'

'Precisely that, Mr Lyminster.'

'Oh, Tickey-Tockey. Well, actually, I was talking to my beloved sis this morning on that very subject. Incidentally, are you sure we shouldn't be letting Twinks in on this confab? She's got a brainbox the size of Westminster Hall – with the rest of the House of Commons thrown in.'

'The fact remains, Mr Lyminster, that your sister was not a witness to the criminal event which took place at the Pocket Theatre last night. Therefore, she has nothing of relevance to tell us.'

'No, but she's the panda's panties when it comes to all the logic and deduction stuff you were talking about.'

'I think, Mr Lyminster,' the detective said, with some *hauteur*, 'you will find that my experience in the business of deduction will be quite adequate to deal with the current enquiry.'

'Fair biddles. I just thought—'

'So, Mr Lyminster,' Dewar continued forcefully, 'what conclusions did you and your *highly talented* sister come up with, as to who might have been responsible for the abduction?'

'Well, I'm a bit of an empty revolver when it comes to that kind of rombooley, but Twinks did flush out the partridge that Whiffler might be being held to ransom. But she said the chock in the cogwheel there was that there hadn't been a ransom note.'

'I think what your *amazingly gifted* sister was saying,' suggested the Inspector, his sarcasm getting stronger by the minute, 'was that you weren't aware of there being a ransom note.'

'Not quite sure what you—'

'I know it's always difficult for *amateur sleuths* . . .' sarcasm now slapped on with a distemper brush '. . . to understand that the police do have certain advantages over them . . . like having access to relevant evidence. A ransom note was left at the stage door of the Pocket Theatre.'

'Was it, by Cheddar!'

'And an identical one was delivered last night to the Earl of Hartlepool at Little Tickling.'

'Well, I'll be kippered like a herring! I'd give a millionaire's wallet to know what's in that note.'

'How fortunate then that you're talking to me, Mr Lyminster.' Smugly, the Inspector drew a folded sheet of paper out of his overcoat pocket. 'Obviously, this is not the original, just a copy, but it might entertain you to have a look at it.'

Blotto took the proffered note and read the following:

'IF YOU WANT TO SEE YOUR SON ALIVE AGAIN, IT'LL COST YOU A HUNDRED THOUSAND POUNDS. YOU WILL SHORTLY BE GIVEN INSTRUCTIONS ON HOW TO MAKE THE PAYMENT.'

'Biscuits!' said Blotto. And he meant it. 'So, has the aged Earl stumped up the spondulicks?'

'No. This, Mr Lyminster, is where the case becomes rather unusual . . . and indeed why I am seeking your help.'

'Seeking my help?'

'Yes. You know the Earl of Hartlepool, I believe?'

'Yes, met the old fossil a few times when I went up to Little Tickling to turn out for Whiffler's estate cricket team.'

'I would be grateful, Mr Lyminster, if you could make another trip up to Shropshire, as soon as possible.'

'Well, I could do. No icing off my cake. But why?'

'To persuade the Earl to take this ransom note seriously.'

'Sorry, old thimble. Not on the same page.'

'I spoke to the Earl of Hartlepool this morning . . .'

'Good for you.'

'. . . to check whether he had received his copy of the ransom note.'

'And had the old warthog?'

'Yes, he had.'

'Then everything is all tiddle and pom, isn't it?'

'No. Everything is far from what you call "tiddle and pom". The Earl's response when he read the note, which, as you will recall, began, "IF YOU WANT TO SEE YOUR SON ALIVE AGAIN . . .".'

'Yes, of course I recall that,' said Blotto, who didn't like having aspersions cast on his short-term memory.

'The Earl's response was: "I'm actually not that bothered about seeing my son again."'

'Broken biscuits,' said Blotto. And he only said that when things were really serious.

6

A Peer of the Realm

The first thing to be said about Little Tickling is that it was extremely big. The Earl of Hartlepool's estate did actually take up most of Shropshire, and the stately home at the centre of it had been built to scale. The original structure, a castle, complete with moat and drawbridge, had been built soon after the Norman Conquest. To this, over the years, had been added, in a broad selection of architectural styles, multiple wings and extensions. At various times over the building's history, various estate managers and other functionaries had begun an inventory of the number of rooms the premises contained, but all had given up, round the two hundred mark, from sheer exhaustion.

Unlike many stately piles – Tawcester Towers, to name but one – Little Tickling was in an extraordinarily good state of repair. The rents the Earl of Hartlepool received, from properties in the vast swathes of central London that he owned, ensured that money was never a problem, in any area of his life. So, to pay out a hundred thousand to the abductors of his son would be no more than a fleabite. The reason for his unwillingness to stump up the old jingle-jangle, therefore, must have lain elsewhere.

Twinks, who had quickly winkled out of Blotto the truth about the ransom note, was determined to find out that reason.

They drove up the next morning in the Lagonda. It was a delightful spring day, so they had the hood down. Though Blotto took the wheel, they did bring Corky Froggett along with them. This pleased the chauffeur enormously. Not only because it offered another opportunity for him to serve and – always a possibility – perhaps to lay down his life for the young master, but also because Little Tickling held another attraction for him. On previous visits to the ancestral pile, he had formed a close acquaintanceship with one of the parlour maids called Rosie. And seeing Rosie again was a very appealing prospect. (Though the one true love of Corky Froggett's life had been Yvette in war-torn France, he had always been a man of a practical nature, ready to explore the possibilities of the second best.)

When they entered the main gates of Little Tickling, they still had two miles of drive to traverse before they reached the house, and it was then, as the noise of the main roads receded, that Twinks started to interrogate her brother.

'You know Whiffler well, don't you?'

'As well as I know the handle of my cricket bat.'

'And would you say that there had ever been any antagonism between him and his father?'

'No, I'd never say that.'

'Why not?'

'Because I don't know what "antagonism" means.'

'Ah. Well, to take the thing down to its frilly drawers, did you ever see them getting angry with each other? Did Whiffler and his Aged P often disagree about things?'

'Good ticket,' said Blotto. 'On the same page now. Oh yes; in fact, shuffling through the old memory cards, I can't remember a single thing on which they did agree.'

'Did they actually argue?'

'Like a pair of cats shut in the same dustbin.'

'And what were their arguments about?'

'Oh, everything under the umbrella, really. But what really got them going shovel and poker was the inheritance.'

'What, you mean all this?' Twinks gestured to the rolling hills of the Little Tickling estate.

'That too, but particularly the actual Earldom.'

'What do you mean, Blotters? Come on, uncage the ferrets.'

'Well, as you know, Twinks me old steam bath, the Earl is an Earl.'

'With you so far, bro.'

'And when he tumbles off the trailer, Whiffler, as his only son, will become the Earl.'

'Tickey-Tockey.'

'The Earl of Hartlepool.'

'Yes, I know which one.'

'But Whiffler doesn't want to do that.'

'Ah.'

'He's very happy with his life as it's currently trickling along, thank you very much. So long as he's got enough of the old jingle-jangle to lunch at the Gren and take the odd actress out for dinner, he's as happy as a duck in orange. Never one to stick his head out of the trenches, Whiffler, he hates the idea of being pointed out to everyone as an Earl. And the prospect of having to take a seat in the House of Lords, along with all the other fossils ... well, that appeals to him about as much as a car tyre does to a hedge-hog. So, he keeps saying his Aged P should change his will and pass the title on to the next in line, but the Pater won't hear of it.'

'And who is the next in line?'

'A solicitor living in Croydon.'

Twinks could not suppress a patrician shudder. 'Well, you can see the Earl's point, can't you?'

'Oh, I agree. The thought of that kind of oikish sponge-worm sitting in the House of Lords ...' Blotto's shudder matched his sister's. 'They'll be letting in Socialists next.'

* * *

The Earl of Hartlepool's face was as pale as his son's was red. His body was as thin as Whiffler's was bulky. The tweed suit hung around him like a dustsheet on a lectern. Tufts of white hair stuck out at random angles from his cranium. His nose was smudged with what might have been ink, and his hands were encrusted with some yellowish compound.

The huge space into which the Little Tickling butler ushered Blotto and Twinks had once been one of Little Tickling's ballrooms, but now appeared to have been converted into a carpenter's workshop. Dusty portraits, displays of weaponry and ancient shotguns hinted at its previous use, but now tools hung from hooks on the walls, and everything (including the Earl) was covered with a thin layer of sawdust. On a small brazier bubbled a pot of something whose smell identified it as hoof glue.

And on the massive workbench stood the artefact, on which the Earl was working with such manic intensity that he did not notice the new arrivals. Though far from finished – there were still over a hundred rooms to go – it was recognisable as a model of the stately home in which they stood, Little Tickling in miniature. And from the piles of components on the workbench, it was clear that the model was made of matchsticks.

The butler, who gloried in the name of Pentecost, cleared his throat with that smooth finesse which only very experienced butlers can achieve, and the noble Earl looked up.

'Well, fiddle my faddle,' he said. 'Visitors?'

'Yes, milord,' said Pentecost.

'Why the devil have you let them in?'

'They are Devereux and Honoria Lyminster, and their father was the Duke of Tawcester.'

'Ah.'

'And I have always understood, milord, that you wish me always to admit genuine aristocrats into the house.'

'Oh, very well,' said the Earl, without enthusiasm. 'You can go, Pentecost.'

'Yes, milord.' The butler paused by the door. 'Would it be appropriate, milord, for me to offer your guests some refreshment?'

'Heavens, no, Pentecost. Start doing that, and they'll never leave.'

'Very good, milord.' The butler melted into the corridor.

The Earl continued to take no notice of his guests, pre-occupied with affixing, with hoof glue and a pair of tweezers, another matchstick to what was clearly the cupola above the Little Tickling entrance hall. Once he had got that in place to his satisfaction, he looked round for his next building block, and found he had run out. He picked up a matchbox bearing the insignia of an upmarket pipe-maker which operated in an arcade off Jermyn Street, and shook out its contents. With a scalpel he began to cut off the heads of the matches, discarding the flammable parts to join thousands of others in a large wooden crate beside his workbench.

Blotto cleared his throat, aware that he wasn't doing it as well as Pentecost had. But the sound did at least make the Earl look up briefly. 'Oh,' he said, before returning to his matchsticks and scalpel. 'You still here?'

'Yes.'

'Why?'

'Erm. We actually have met before,' Blotto ventured.

'Have we? No recollection of it. I can't be expected to remember every Tom, Dick and Harry, you know.'

'I'm actually not a Tom, or a Dick, or a Harry. I'm a Lyminster.'

'Are you, by thunder?'

'Tickey-Tockey. Your son Giles and I were muffin-toasters at Eton.'

'Were you, by lightning?'

'Yes. I often used to come here to play cricket with him.'

This did finally seem to penetrate the aged peer's con-sciousness. 'Oh yes, I know who you are. Potto.'

'Blotto.'

'Blotto, yes. I remember you. Thick as a dungeon wall.'

'Oh, thank you, milord.'

'Here for the cricket, are you? Is it the cricket season already?'

'No, milord.'

Twinks had been silent for much longer than was her custom. She now burst out with: 'We're here because your son Giles has been abducted.'

'Yes, I heard about that.' The noble peer, completely unperturbed, turned back to his matchsticks and tweezers.

'And we,' Twinks persisted, 'are determined to find him and set him free.'

'That shouldn't be too difficult ... that is, assuming that you have a spare hundred thou.'

'Ah, well, that's a bit of a fly in the woodpile,' said Blotto. 'You see, because of the plumbing.'

'Plumbing?'

'Yes, milord. The Tawcester Towers plumbing.'

'I don't know what you're talking about, Blotto, though I do remember you better with every word you say. It all comes back – you never had anything between the ears. A total void.'

'Oh, thank you, milord.'

'I think there's one pointette that should be made,' said Twinks. 'Even if we did have a spare hundred thou ...'

'Which we don't,' Blotto asserted.

'... the fact is that the ransom note was addressed to you, milord. You are Giles's father, and don't you believe that certain responsibilities come along with that role?'

'Young lady, responsibility is a two-way process. If my wastrel of a son showed any sense of responsibility about the title which he should by rights inherit, then I might feel some responsibility to get him out of his current plight. Since he has shown no desire to become the Earl of Hartlepool – and has indeed expressed his deep unwilling-ness to take on the honour ... well, I've washed my hands of him.'

'But hasn't it occurred to you that he might be in danger?'

Blotto came in quickly to support his sister's argument. 'Yes. I saw the boddoes who abducted him. There were two of them – no, three; well, at least three – and they looked to be total lumps of toadspawn. They were carrying guns.'

'Then I definitely don't want to have anything to do with them.'

'Sorry? Not on the same page.'

'I don't believe in shooting.'

'No, I agree. Shooting people is way beyond the barbed wire.'

'I didn't say "people". I don't believe in shooting anything.'

'What?' Blotto gestured to the shotguns on the wall. 'What, not even taking one of those out on the estate and blasting away at the odd pheasant?'

'No.'

'Partridge?'

'No.'

'Grouse?'

'No.'

'Ptarmigan?'

'No.'

Twinks felt she should intervene before the entire avian population of the world had been catalogued. 'The point is, milord,' she said, 'that your attitude to shooting is not what's important here. It's the attitude to shooting of the stenchers who've abducted Whiffler that matters.'

'Whiffler?' echoed the bemused Earl.

'That's what Giles was known as by all his muffin-toasters at Eton,' Blotto explained.

'Why?'

'I can't remember. Though it might have been something to do with a noise he made.'

'What kind of noise?'

'A whiffling noise.'

'And when did he make this whiffling noise?'

'I can't remember.'

'Anyway, forget that,' said Twinks. 'The pointette I'm trying to make, milord, is that Giles is in serious danger. The ransom note bullied off with: "IF YOU WANT TO SEE YOUR SON ALIVE AGAIN . . ." The running sores who're holding him have got guns. If you make no response to their note, they're quite capable of coffinating him.'

The Earl of Hartlepool shrugged. 'That's a risk Giles has to take. He got himself into this particular gluepot. He must find his way out.'

Having been brought up in the untender care of the Dowager Duchess, Twinks did not expect to encounter parental sentimentality anywhere, but she did think the Earl was going a bit far in this case. Leaving one's son to be murdered by gun-toting desperadoes did not comply with her reading of the rules of *noblesse oblige*.

'Milord, you can't play the rat's part with Giles,' she protested. 'He is blood of your blood.'

'Is he, though? Blood of my blood wouldn't talk of renouncing the Earldom. Blood of my blood would do anything to prevent the title going to *a solicitor in Croydon*.' He was as appalled by the thought of this subspecies as Blotto and Twinks had been.

'I'm sure Giles would be persuaded to see reason.'

'Do you think so?'

'But only if he's alive. If he's shot dead by his kidnappers, he won't be able to see anything, let alone reason.'

'Huh. If I believed that, I would do something to save him. But I know Giles too well. Once he's got an idea fixed in his brain, nothing'll shift it.'

'I'm convinced he could be persuaded.'

'By whom?' The Earl's focus returned to his matchstick model.

'I could persuade him!' said Twinks passionately.

This outburst made the peer of the realm actually look at her for the first time. And clearly, like all men, he very much liked what he saw.

'I say, you're a fine, frolicsome filly. Yes, I see anyone of the male gender might be persuaded by *you*.'

Twinks pressed home her advantage. 'I'd put my last laddered silk stocking on the fact that I could persuade Giles to take on the Earldom.'

'Hm. Interesting. The thing is, though, that I actually have another plan.'

'Oh. What's that when it's got its spats on?' asked Blotto.

'That I should remarry.'

'Toad-in-the-hole!' said Blotto.

'Yes,' said the Earl. 'I think it's a particularly fruity wheeze. I remarry, having found the right filly, of course, have another son; then, when I take the old one-way ticket, he becomes the Earl of Hartlepool.' He looked closely at Twinks. 'What did you say your name was?'

'Honoria Lyminster.'

'Ah. Well, I wonder if you—'

He was interrupted by the sound of a telephone ringing. He picked up the receiver from its cradle, blew the dust off it and said, 'Hello? Earl of Hartlepool.'

Blotto and Twinks could hear nothing from the other end of the line, only his responses. 'In a what? Suitcase, yes. Telephone box? Behind the Pocket Theatre? A hundred thousand by midnight tomorrow night? Otherwise, my son . . . ? I understand. Yes, well, thank you for the information, but I'm afraid I'm not going to do business with you. I have thought of another solution to my problem. Goodbye.' And he replaced the receiver in its cradle.

Twinks couldn't stop herself from saying, 'You shouldn't have done that! You should have kept them on the line till we get the police to trace the—'

'Oh, fiddlesticks,' said the Earl of Hartlepool.

'You said,' Blotto prompted cautiously, 'that you'd got another solution to your problem . . . ?'

'Yes,' said the Earl. 'Damned good one.' He turned to Twinks and asked, 'Will you marry me?'

7

Dinner after the Show – I

'A hundred thou by tomorrow night,' said Blotto, with a low whistle. 'Or Whiffler gets coffinated. Any thoughts how we might get our mitts on the jingle-jangle?'

'No,' said Twinks, uncharacteristically subdued.

Blotto had allowed Corky Froggett to drive back to London, so he and Twinks could sit in the back of the Lagonda and really focus on their Whiffler Rescue Plan. Which was currently somewhat undernourished. Or, not to put too fine a point on it, non-existent.

'I was thinking,' said Blotto, 'that tomorrow night, we should stake out the telephone box behind the old Pocket Theatre, and nab the four-faced filchers when they come to pick up the mazuma.'

'Don't you think they'll be anticipating that?'

'They may be, but don't don your worry-boots about that. I'll have my cricket bat with me.' A cloud of uncertainty crossed his noble brow. 'At least, I think I'll have my cricket bat with me. Corky,' he called out, 'is my cricket bat packed in the car boot?'

'No, milord. It's back at Tawcester Towers.'

'Oh, that's a stye in the eye! I say, Corky old fellow, would you mind driving back to the homestead tomorrow to pick the spoffing thing up?'

'I'll do better than that, milord. The minute we get back

to the Savoy, I'll go straight down to Tawcester Towers and have the bat back before midnight.'

'You know, Corky,' said Blotto, 'you're a Grade A foundation stone.'

'Hello?'

Blotto had rung through the moment he got back to his suite. He didn't recognise the voice at the other end of the line. 'Is that Scotland Yard?' he asked.

'Scotland Yard?' There was almost a giggle in the unknown voice. 'Oh yes, right, right. This is Scotland Yard, yes.'

'Could I speak to Detective Inspector Craig Dewar?'

'Of course. Reg, some geyser wants to talk to Detective Inspector Craig Dewar.'

There was a moment of silence, then the Inspector's familiar voice came on the line. 'Yes, Mr Lyminster. What can I do to help you?'

'Well, I've got some information,' said Blotto.

'Did you travel to Little Tickling to see the Earl?'

'Certainly did.'

'And he has by now been given instructions about where to put the money?'

'Good ticket. We were actually there when the ping from the kidnappers came through.'

'We? Who's we?'

'Me and my old sis, Twinks.'

'I thought we agreed that this investigation was a secret just between you and me.'

'No probs there. Twinks doesn't know I'm in touch with you.'

'Very well.' But the Inspector didn't sound completely happy as he said the words. 'More importantly, though, has the Earl agreed to pay the money?'

'Ah. Now this is where there's a bit of a kink in the fly-line.' And Blotto proceeded to tell the Inspector about the noble peer's intransigence (though he didn't use the word 'intransigence', because he'd never heard of it) about paying for his son's release.

'That's very unfortunate, Mr Lyminster. These desperadoes have threatened to kill Mr Tortington, and I don't think they're the kind to make idle threats.'

'So, you think they'd actually be prepared to coffinate Whiffler?'

'If they don't get the money by midnight tomorrow, I'm sure that's exactly what they will do.'

'You sound as if you know who the stenchers are, Inspector.'

'We may be close to identifying them,' Dewar responded cautiously. Then he went all official. 'But I'm afraid it is not Scotland Yard policy to discuss an investigation in progress.'

'Take that on board, Inspector. But I should tell you that my sister and I had a real buzzbanger of an idea.'

'Oh?'

'Well, these four-faced filchers are expecting the old jingle-jangle to be placed in this telephone box behind the Pocket Theatre . . .'

'Yes.'

'So we thought, if we staked out the telephone box, we'd snap the lumps of toadspawn when they came snuffling for the loot.'

'And hasn't it occurred to you, Mr Lyminster, that the kidnappers might be armed? They'll have guns.'

'Don't get into crimps over that, Inspector. I'll have my cricket bat.'

'Hm. Mr Lyminster, what you don't seem to have taken into account is that I am conducting an official police investigation here.'

'Yes, don't worry, I read your semaphore.'

'And it doesn't seem to have occurred to you that we might have thought of staking out the telephone box to apprehend the villains. So I very much advise you – and your sister – not to go near that telephone box tomorrow.'

'But I—'

'Remember, Mr Lyminster, my team at Scotland Yard are the official investigators here. You and your sister are just *amateurs*.'

Ouch. The Inspector really knew how to hurt.

When Twinks got back to her suite after the excursion to Little Tickling, Reception rang through with a message for her. Jack Carmichael wondered whether she might be free to dine with him after the evening's performance of *Light and Frothy*. If so, they could meet at the restaurant.

She thought back to their dinner of the night before, when Jack had so charmingly talked about his profession, and the hard work of rehearsal that went into creating such an apparently effortless confection as *Light and Frothy*. She remembered the compliments to her, which he had slipped so randomly into their conversation.

But, above all, she remembered Jack Carmichael's sheer gorgeousness. To sit opposite, bathing in the brown-eyed adoration of such a beautiful man, was a pleasure of which she could not get enough.

Twinks decided she would be free.

As specified by the Savoy Reception, Jack Carmichael had booked the same restaurant they had gone to the previous night. Twinks was already there when he arrived. The star was warmly greeted by the maître d', and the waiting staff made a great fuss of him. In his regular alcove, there were three signed photographs of him on the wall. He ordered exactly the same cocktail, food and wine as he had the night before. He was clearly a creature of habit.

Twinks wouldn't have minded that, but for the fact that his conversation was also identical to that of the night before. What had seemed so charming when first heard became, by reiteration, rather dull. Her appreciation of his clipped upper-class drawl gave way to the conviction that he hadn't been born to such vowels. Twinks knew enough genuine aristocrats to recognise what wasn't the genuine article.

She also realised another thing she hadn't on their first meeting: that, basically, Jack Carmichael's conversation was all about Jack Carmichael. Though he still slipped in the odd compliment to her (word for word the same as the previous night's), he talked for at least forty-five minutes about that evening's performance of *Light and Frothy*, examining in minute detail the way he'd played each song, dance and sketch. Eventually, he turned to Twinks with an engagingly boyish grin and said, 'Still, enough about me. What did *you* think of the way I sang "Mist Over Mayfair": you know, the song that closed the first half?'

Any illusions about there being a future in their relationship having quickly dissipated, Twinks didn't want to waste time. And she realised that she was sitting opposite someone who knew the whole *Light and Frothy* set-up inside out. If romance wasn't going to work out – and it clearly wasn't – then she might as well take the opportunity to pursue her investigation into Giles 'Whiffler' Tortington's abduction.

'Tell me,' she said brusquely, not answering Jack Carmichael's question, 'about Frou-Frou Gavotte.'

He looked suitably dumbfounded. He wasn't used to the idea of talking about other people. After a silence, he replied, 'Well, she's obviously very fortunate.'

'Fortunate? Why?'

'Well, she's in a show with me. Getting her name beside mine on the marquee outside the Pocket Theatre can only help her career.'

'Are you suggesting the poor little droplet is not as famous as you are?'

He laughed at the sheer incongruity of the question. 'Of

course she isn't. Now, you know that tap dance I do in the "London is for Lovers" routine—'

'I'm not interested in that. You told me all about it last night.'

'Ah yes, but tonight I put in a slight variation on the—'

'Oh, stuff a pillow in it, Jack! I'm not interested in you.'

Having never heard these words before from anyone, Jack Carmichael's face took on the look of a barrage balloon pierced by enemy fire. He was still too shocked to speak, so Twinks went on, 'I want to talk about Frou-Frou. Whiffler had fallen for her like an inebriated scaffolder. He was even talking of the two of them twiddling up the old reef-knot. Well, that might have put lumps in someone's custard. I'm just wondering whose.'

'"Whiffler"? What is "Whiffler"?'

'Giles Tortington, son and heir to the Earl of Hartlepool. Haven't you noticed he's been coming to see Frou-Frou practically every night?'

'Oh, I never notice people like that. I can't be expected to tell the Stage-Door Johnnies apart.'

'Well, let's line up the pot-shot from another angle. I can't imagine someone who looks like Frou-Frou has the nature of a nun.'

'What do you mean?'

'Oh, do try to keep up, Jack! Don't be a total voidbrain. I'm suggesting that Frou-Frou Gavotte must have had other bees buzzing round her honeypot.' He still looked blank. 'That she's had other admirers!'

Finally, Jack Carmichael got the point. 'Oh, good heaven, yes! Frou-Frou's been passed around like a salt cellar. There can't be an actor in London – well, an actor in London who's interested in that kind of thing – who hasn't had a taste of Frou-Frou.'

'What about boddoes outside the theatre?'

'I'm sure she's had her fair share of them too. I mean, the girl was brought up in the gutter. No breeding at all.'

'Unlike you?' said Twinks contentiously. Breeding was a subject about which she knew a fair wallop.

'I went to public school, you know.' He mentioned a name.

'*Minor* public school,' Twinks observed dismissively. 'And in Scotland. What did your father do?'

Jack Carmichael smiled with some pride. 'He was a solicitor.'

So far as Twinks was concerned, that said it all. She would have left immediately, but for the fact that she still wanted to do further picking of the actor's brain (if, she wondered, that wasn't too grandiose a description of the organ in question). 'I was asking about Frou-Frou's boyfriends outside the theatre . . .'

'Wouldn't you rather talk about the American accent I used in the sketch *Cowboy, Cowgirl*?'

'No,' said Twinks coldly. 'Come on, uncage the ferrets! Boyfriends outside the theatre?'

Jack Carmichael was by now too cowed to argue. 'I really don't have any names,' he said. 'But I know, in the early days of rehearsal for *Light and Frothy*, Frou-Frou used to be picked up at the end of the day by someone in a large black saloon.'

'Did you ever see the stencher?' asked Twinks, who had no doubts that they were talking about a villain.

'No. The car was just parked outside the front of the theatre. On the few occasions when Frou-Frou and I came out together after we'd finished rehearsals, the car would be there, and she just let herself in.'

'Front seat or back?'

'Back.'

'And you never saw anyone get out of the car?'

'No.'

'And you didn't see who was inside?'

'No. The jolly old thing had tinted windows.'

Twinks was thoughtful. According to Blotto's account, the car in which Whiffler had been abducted also had

65

tinted windows. And there weren't many vehicles in London which boasted that feature. 'Hm,' she said. 'You don't happen to know when Frou-Frou and Whiffler started sharing an umbrella, do you?'

'As I said, I'm not particularly interested in the doings of Stage-Door Johnnies.'

'Do you remember whether she had any special guests at the First Night?'

'I actually do,' Jack replied. 'Because, at the time,' he continued with some pride, 'I had an aristocratic admirer who was going to be in the audience.'

'Oh? And who was she?'

'Baroness Godalming,' he announced dramatically.

'Only a Baroness,' came the icy reply. 'Anyway, what in the name of strawberries does this minor aristocrat have to do with Frou-Frou Gavotte?'

'Ah. Well, I mentioned before the First Night that the Baroness would be there, and Frou-Frou said, "Ooh, I'm going to have an aristocratic admirer out there, and all."' The impersonation of his fellow performer was cruelly accurate.

'So, that might well have been Whiffler . . . assuming that she didn't make a habit of mingling with the peerage.'

'She would have done, if she had got the opportunity. Frou-Frou's always had an eye to the main chance. She can smell money like a truffle hound.'

'Hm. Anything else you remember that might be relevant?'

'Relevant to what?'

'Relevant to the business of rescuing "Whiffler" Tortington from his abductors.'

'Oh.' He was put out. 'Is that why you agreed to have dinner with me – to help your investigation?'

'No, I agreed to have dinner with you because I thought we might have an interesting evening. When it became clear that that particular dish was not on the menu, I took the opportunity to further my investigation.' Her explanation did not make Jack Carmichael look much happier. 'Come on, don't shuffle round the shrubbery. Anything else you remember from the First Night?'

'Well, just before the show opened that night, I was by the stage door with Pierre Labouze . . . he's the producer of *Light and Frothy*. Have you met him?'

'No, but my brother has.'

'Well, we were there when a special delivery arrived for Frou-Frou.'

'What was it?'

'Just a brown envelope, with her name on it. I assumed it was another Good Luck card. But the envelope hadn't been sealed very well and, as the stage doorman handled it, something dropped out.'

'What?'

'A bullet.'

Twinks's azure eyes sparkled. 'Give that pony a rosette,' she murmured.

'And Pierre – Pierre Labouze, that is, said, "It serves the silly *vache* right. She should be more careful about the company she keeps."'

'And did he offer any further explanation for what he said?'

Jack Carmichael shook his head.

'Maybe I should have a wordette with Pierre Labouze.'

'Good luck with that.'

'What do you mean?'

'Just that our estimable producer is not easy to contact. He has no telephone. He allows no one near his rehearsals. He does not even do press interviews. If you try to make contact with him, I can guarantee you will fail in the attempt.'

'Oh?' Twinks was confident of her ability to winkle out even the most unsociable of molluscs. 'Surely I can find him at the Pocket Theatre?'

'He won't speak to you.'

'But he speaks to you. He speaks to the cast of his shows.'

'Yes, but only on matters of work. Pierre Labouze is completely dedicated to his work. He watches every performance of every show he produces. Every evening he's in the theatre half an hour before the curtain goes up. Every evening – however well the performance has gone – he comes round to our dressing rooms with notes for us. Pierre's only interest is improving what he always calls "A Pierre Labouze Revue". Nothing else matters to him.'

'Isn't he susceptible to feminine charms?' asked Twinks, with a confidence born of the long catalogue of men who had fallen for her like deckchairs in a hurricane.

'Not any feminine charms. Not even yours. He's totally obsessed by his revues. Pierre Labouze would only speak to you if he thought you had the potential to become the next Frou-Frou Gavotte.'

'Oh?' Twinks looked gratified. 'Well, I can warble a bit, and trip the light fantastic.'

'However well you did that, Pierre Labouze would not be interested.'

'No?'

'No, you were born with far too much silver spoon in your mouth. Pierre likes dragging girls up from the gutter to create stars of them. Like the Piggy person that *modern* playwright Bernard Shaw wrote about.' When someone like Jack Carmichael used the word 'modern' in connection to matters theatrical, it was not a compliment.

'*Pygmalion?*' Twinks suggested.

'That's the cove. Chap who makes a statue come to life. That's how Pierre Labouze sees himself. Making silk purses out of sows' ears. He doesn't like real aristocrats, he gets a thrill out of *creating* his own aristocrats.'

'Jollissimo,' murmured Twinks, seeing clearly what the next step in her investigation should be. She gathered up her sequinned reticule. 'Thank you, Jack – for the dinner, if not for your incredibly monotonous and solipsistic conversation. I don't think you have any more information that will be of use to me.'

And she swept out of the restaurant, with the poise of an Elizabethan galleon watching the last remains of the Spanish Armada wrecking themselves on the coast of Ireland.

Her departure left the maître d' and the rest of the staff open-mouthed with astonishment. No woman had ever walked out on Jack Carmichael before. The revue star's stock could not have diminished more rapidly if he had been heard speaking in his native Scottish accent.

8

Dinner after the Show – II

Blotto would have been embarrassed if Twinks knew what he was up to, but she had told him she was meeting Jack Carmichael at the restaurant rather than the Pocket Theatre, so he knew the coast would be clear. As soon as she'd left for her assignation, he had telephoned the stage door to see if Dolly Diller might be free to join him for dinner after that night's performance of *Light and Frothy*. He was gratified to receive a message soon after that she would be delighted to be his guest.

He was not the only man in evening wear loitering outside the stage door. Though he recognised the others for what they were – Stage-Door Johnnies – it never occurred to him that he was now a member of their ranks.

He had asked Reception at the Savoy to recommend somewhere for him and his guest to dine and, perhaps unsurprisingly, they had suggested the Savoy Grill. Blotto thought it was very clever of them to name somewhere so close to where he was, and only a short drive from the Pocket Theatre. He notified Corky Froggett when he wanted the Lagonda outside the Savoy's main entrance.

Dolly Diller looked stunning as she emerged from the stage door. Despite the warmth of the late spring evening, she was draped in a white fox-fur coat, which immediately made Blotto feel jealous. He felt sure she hadn't bought the garment herself, and he already wanted to take his cricket bat to the stencher who'd bought it for her.

But he restrained the instinct, and was rewarded by an "Ello, darlin'!" and – even better – a big sloppy kiss, which left a rose of lipstick on his cheek.

Corky Froggett was standing by the car's back door. His face was impassive as he opened it to admit the young master and his guest. Blotto was not entirely pleased that, before she got in, Dolly Diller gave the chauffeur an "Ello, darlin'!" and a big sloppy kiss as well.

Corky too was left with a rose of lipstick. It reminded him of the marks Yvette used to leave on his cheek back in those heady days of wartime.

Blotto was modest by nature. That modesty had been engendered and encouraged by his upbringing in the English aristocracy and the public school system. Boddoes of his breeding didn't talk about themselves. Doing so was a bit beyond the barbed wire. If one of his muffin-toasters at Eton started talking about himself, that could very easily cross over the line into bragging. And bragging was a very small step from that most heinous of crimes amongst the English upper classes – and something to which foreigners (particularly Americans) were unforgivably prone – 'showing off'.

So, Blotto was very unaccustomed to being asked as much about himself as he was by Dolly Diller. He supposed it was flattering, but it was also a bit embarrassing. 'You don't want to know about me,' he kept saying. 'I'm about as interesting as a nun's diary.'

'Oh, you do yourself down,' she kept saying, in that wonderful throaty Cockney gurgle. 'You're the most interesting man I've ever met. Now you tell me about . . .'

Then she was off on another question. She wanted to know all about his family, where he fitted into it. She wanted to know about the history of the Lyminsters,

71

right back to their arrival in England with William the Conqueror.

And she didn't just ask general questions, pretending interest like some deb at a Hunt Ball. Dolly Diller got very specific. She enquired as to whether the current Duke was single. (Blotto told her that Loofah was married to Sloggo, a wife whom he had so far only managed to impregnate with girls.) Then Dolly wanted to know exactly how big the Tawcester Towers estate was, and what other sources of income the Lyminsters had. And she seemed to be particularly intrigued by what would happen to Blotto's inheritance if his older brother the Duke were to die.

He kept trying to infiltrate questions about her, but Dolly seemed resistant to much disclosure. Blotto had never met a woman who was so selfless; she only seemed to be interested in him.

When he did finally get her on to the subject of her own background, she said, 'I was born near the 'Ackney Marshes, but I scrub up all right. I'm an actress, see. I can do voices. If I 'ad to be a Duchess in a play, you wouldn't be able to tell me from the real thing. Listen.' And she went into her toff's version of '"The rain in Spain stays mainly in the plain." There, I sound like every Duchess you ever 'eard, don't I, Blotto?'

Though in fact she didn't sound like any Duchess he had ever heard, he was far too gallant to say so. Instead, he asked, 'Where is Ackney Marshes?'

'You're 'aving me on, Blotto. You know 'Ackney Marshes. Near Clapton, Leyton, Stratford.'

'Tickey-Tockey,' said Blotto, recognising a word he knew. 'Where Shakespeare came from.'

'Who?'

'Shakespeare.'

'Don't know him. Is he in the "business"?'

'"Business"?'

'Theatre.'

'Good ticket. He's bong in the middle of the theatre. Playwright.'

'Oh.' Dolly had lost interest. Most playwrights she met were poor, neurotic and not attracted to girls. She changed the subject. 'How was your visit to the Earl of 'Artlepool then?'

Blotto did not think to question how she knew where he had been that day. He just considered it another example of her intuition and caring nature. 'Oh,' he replied ruefully. 'Didn't pot the black on that one, I'm afraid.'

'It's a bit of a slap in the face him not paying the ransom, isn't it?'

'Major damper, yes. He didn't seem to give a tuppenny butterscotch about what might happen to Whiffler.'

'And did you 'ave any other forts about how you might get the money?'

'No, I'm a bit of an empty revolver when it comes to thinking.'

'But your sister's brighter, ain't she?'

'Oh, Tickey-Tockey, yes. Though even Twinks isn't going to find a hundred thou down the back of the sofa, is she?'

'Pity. And what's Little Tickling like?'

'Massive spread, you know.'

'Earl of 'Artlepool's quite well-'eeled, innie?'

'Yes. For him, a hundred thou would be a couple of grains of sand from a five-mile beach.'

'Maybe the kidnappers should've asked for more . . . ?' Dolly Diller mused.

'Don't think it would have made a groat's-worth of difference. The old fossil has no intention of doing anything to pull Whiffler out of the treacle pot.'

'What's the security like at Little Tickling?' asked Dolly, with another of her abrupt changes of subject.

'Security? Sorry, not reading your semaphore . . . ?'

'I mean, Blotto, did you find it easy getting in?'

'Oh yes. Just pongled up to the front door, pulled the old bell-pull, and Pentecost the butler let us in.'

'And was he the only person guarding the place?'

'Well, there must've been other staff around, but we didn't see any. Pentecost wasn't really *guarding* the place, anyway. People like us don't really guard our places – except during wars, obviously. Tawcester Towers had quite big garrisons during the Wars of the Roses and the Civil War, of course, but not now. We *know* the kind of people who're likely to pop round, so we never lock the doors.'

'So, anyone who wanted to,' asked Dolly ingenuously, 'could just walk into somewhere like Little Tickling, with no one trying to stop them?'

'That's about the right size of pyjamas, yes,' said Blotto.

'Thank you. You 'ave been so helpful. Not just a pretty face, are you, Blotto?'

'Don't talk such meringue,' he said, blushing to the roots of his blond thatch.

Dolly Diller looked up at the restaurant clock. It was well after midnight. 'Well, this 'as been lovely, thank you. But I need my beauty sleep.'

Blotto recognised this as a cue for a compliment. He'd never been very good at making them, but now was his moment to put all that right. 'No amount of beauty sleep,' he said, 'could make you beautiful.'

The expression on Dolly's face told him that, once again, he hadn't got the words quite right. 'Oh, biscuits!' he said. 'What I meant was: No amount of beauty sleep could make you *more* beautiful.'

'Well, thank you, kind sir,' said Dolly Diller, with a little bob of the head. But she did give him a slightly strange look.

'Now, shall I order a cab for you?' he asked.

'Don't worry about that, love. I have my own special taxi service.'

Outside the Savoy stood a black saloon with tinted windows. 'Is this your special taxi service?' asked Blotto.

'Of course it is,' Dolly replied. 'Thank you for a lovely evening.'

She kissed him on the cheek and opened the car's back door.

The imprint of her lipstick glowed, as he watched the vehicle disappear up a side street off the Strand. As he did so, he thought the image was familiar, and only then remembered that the night before he'd watched Whiffler disappear in similar circumstances.

For a moment, he had the thought that his friend might have been using the same 'special taxi service' as Dolly Diller, but then he remembered about how Whiffler had been manhandled into that car by men with guns.

No, it was just a coincidence. Very classy, though, thought Blotto, for a girl like Dolly to organise her transport so well.

Delightful creature, he mused. Absolute breathsapper, and a rather fruity brainbox too. For a moment, Blotto allowed his imagination off the leash. Wouldn't it be wonderful if he could get away from all of the Araminta fffrench-Wyndeaus of this world? They were so affected, so unreal. But teamed up with someone of Dolly Diller's earthy appeal, the prospect of marriage lost much of its ghastliness.

Why shouldn't he and Dolly have a future together? Someone like her would bring a bit of life into the dank corridors of Tawcester Towers. He fantasised about introducing her to Mephistopheles, having her watching from the Pavilion when he led out the estate cricket team. He imagined . . .

But suddenly the image of the Dowager Duchess appeared in his mind, instantly to eclipse all of his hopes and dreams.

Still, he could continue to enjoy Dolly Diller's company, at least till he was inescapably manacled to Araminta fffrench-Wyndeau.

It struck Blotto that the thing he really liked about Dolly, apart from her looks and her brain, was her level of interest in him. He'd never met a woman who had asked him so many questions.

9

Twinks Undercover

It was a happy accident that, just after saying his fond farewell to Dolly Diller, Blotto was in the hotel lobby, just at the moment Twinks stormed in. Long familiarity, from the nursery onward, with her facial expressions, told him that his sister was not a happy hedgehog.

It was only when they were up in her suite, drinking Room Service cocoa (rather in the way they might in her boudoir back at Tawcester Towers), that he dared ask what had put lumps in her custard.

'A man!' she replied. 'A fumacious man!'

'Has somebody been making improper advances to you, sis? Because, if they have, I'll get my spoffing cricket bat and I'll beat the stencher to within a—'

'No, no. Nothing to do with improper advances. Anyway, I can deal with them, as easy as swatting a mozzy. No, what I came up against this evening was blind, self-centred arrogance.'

'Toad-in-the-hole!' said Blotto. 'May I ask who the lump of toadspawn in question is?'

'Jack Carmichael.'

'Oh, the triller and tapster from *Light and Frothy*.'

'You're bong on the nose there, Blotters.'

'But I thought you thought he was the lark's larynx. Supposed to be catnip for the fillies, I'd heard.'

'Yes, his looks come straight off Mount Olympus.'

'He's craggy, you mean?' asked Blotto, who, despite the efforts of the beaks at Eton, had limited knowledge of Greek mythology.

'No, I mean he's as tasty as a dish of strawberries. If I only had to *look* at him, I'd be rolling on camomile lawns. The trouble is, I had to *listen* to him. And the only subj of his conv is himself.'

'Tough Gorgonzola, old fishcake.'

'I'm afraid Jack Carmichael turned out to be proof of the old saying: "All that glisters is not gold."'

'Surely, Twinks me old cough lozenge, you mean "glitters"?'

'No. "Glisters". That's how it is in the original.'

'And what's this "original" when it's got its spats on?'

'It's *The Merchant of Venice.*'

'Spoffing typical of this day and age, isn't it? Merchants going around making up quotations. You'll have solicitors doing it next. I blame Socialism.'

'No, Blotters. *The Merchant of Venice* is a play. By Shakespeare.'

'Oh.' Blotto had certainly heard of Shakespeare. It's hard to get through an English education at any level without having heard of Shakespeare. And if you went to Eton, you were practically force-fed the stuff. 'So, what you're saying, Twinks me old carpet-beater, is that Shakespeare couldn't spell?'

'Not exactly, Blotto me old fish-gutter. Spelling was different in those days.'

'No, spelling's spelling, and it's either right or wrong.' He was quoting one of his old beaks at Eton, who took a less than liberal attitude to Blotto's approximate approach to the matter. 'There's no two ways about it. Shakespeare wrote "glisters", and it should have been "glitters".'

'As I say, spelling was different back then. I mean, Shakespeare spelled his own name in a number of different ways.'

'The poor droplet couldn't spell his own name? Well, I'll be snickered. But I've been able to spell mine, from a very early age. And mine's very difficult, because it's got a "y" and a silent "x" in it.'

Blotto was hugely gratified. It was not often that he had the sensation of feeling intellectually superior to anyone. And being intellectually superior to Shakespeare ... well, that really was the panda's panties.

'Anyway, I don't want to think any more about that slimer Jack Carmichael. How did you spend your evening, Blotters?'

'Oh, just ate here in the Grill.' This edited version of events came to him quite instinctively. He didn't often keep things from Twinks. She could usually intuit what he'd been up to, anyway. But, for some reason, he didn't at that moment want to share with her his special feelings for Dolly Diller.

'Anyway,' said his sister, 'the one thing I did get out of that self-obsessed blunderhead was what the next step should be in our investigation.'

'Toad-in-the-hole!' said Blotto enthusiastically. 'Is it going to involve me, doing doughty deeds with my cricket bat?'

'No,' replied Twinks, disappointingly in the circumstances.

Blotto and Twinks were both exceptionally good-looking, but their given quota of brains had not been fairly divided. Though Blotto was enviably strong, brave and a demon on the cricket or the hunting field, that was probably the extent of his accomplishments. He certainly had demonstrated no aptitude for the performing skills in which his sister excelled. She played piano to international concert standard, and her skills on the dance floor were yet another talent which reduced heavy-footed scions of aristocratic houses to incoherent adoration.

She had also, unbeknownst even to her brother, over the years built up a wide repertory of voices which she could take on at a moment's notice. This had started with her love of foreign languages. The intellectual achievement of reading and writing them was not sufficient for her ambitious nature, so she also prided herself on being able to speak fluent, perfectly accented French, German, Italian, Spanish, Dutch, Russian, Serbo-Croat, Turkish, Greek (Ancient and Modern), Hebrew, Mandarin, Xhosa, Yoruba, Ashanti, Urdu, Gujarati and most other dialects of the Indian subcontinent (though, by her own confession, her spoken Sanskrit was a bit rough).

But Twinks hadn't limited her voice-learning to foreign languages. She had also perfected most of the regional speech patterns of the British Isles. Needless to say, she didn't restrict herself to such broad generalisations as Scottish, Welsh and Irish. She had mastered the nuances between individual regions. She knew how few fricative consonants an Aberdonian would share with a Glaswegian: she could differentiate Llandovery and Llandrindod Wells; she would never get her Kilkenny mixed up with her Cork. And she would never slip on the treacherous vowels of Londonderry and Newcastle.

So, to decide which accent she required for the job in hand was a matter of moments.

Deciding how she should be dressed for the occasion was another matter entirely. Twinks had a very shrewd estimate of her own considerable skills, but always knew when outside support was needed. And, in this case, she was in no doubt that she had to go the next morning to her favourite couturier, Madame Clothilde of Mayfair.

It was always Madame Clothilde whose advice Twinks would seek on the appropriate apparel for a Hunt Ball, a Coronation or a royal funeral, but the dressmaker had other useful, but less publicly acknowledged, skills. During what Blotto always referred to as 'the recent dust-up in Frogland' (also known as 'the War to End All Wars'), she, as a young French citizen, had achieved remarkable feats of daring behind enemy lines. For these exploits, Clothilde Degazeuze had always been in disguise, totally transforming her teenage self into German civilians, German troopers and German top brass, to sabotage in various ways their military endeavours. Such was her fame for convincing transformations, that some believed it was Clothilde Degazeuze, in disguise, who started the rumours about the Angels of Mons.

In all of her guises, she was working on behalf of France and its allies, with the aim of destroying German munitions and morale. The high spot, at Verdun in 1916, was her impersonation of Kaiser Wilhelm II, when she told his senior officers, in perfect German, that they 'might as well give up because there was no way they had a snowball's chance in hell of winning.'

None of Clothilde Degazeuze's exploits was ever chronicled. The level of secrecy in such operations was so tight that nobody would refer to them, even under torture. And when she opened her exclusive couturier business as Madame Clothilde of Mayfair, no one – except a few superbrains like Twinks – knew anything of her heroic shape-shifting history.

Corky Froggett brought the Lagonda to a serene stop outside the South Audley Street showroom. 'Oooh, I meant to ask you something,' said Twinks.

'Yes, milady?'

'Did you fetch Blotto's cricket bat from Tawcester Towers?'

'Safely in the dickie of the Lag, milady.'

'Splendissimo,' she said as she disembarked. 'I don't know how long I'll be.'

'That is of no consequence, milady. Spend a week in there, and I will still be out here waiting on your pleasure.' If Corky couldn't lay down his life (or at least make that life extraordinarily uncomfortable) for the young master, he was more than happy to make similar sacrifices for the young mistress.

'A couple of hours should be the top of the column,' said Twinks airily. She had, earlier in the morning, tried to contact Pierre Labouze through the Pocket Theatre, but, as Jack Carmichael had predicted, drawn a blank. Which was why she was going down the Madame Clothilde of Mayfair route.

The reinvented, London-based Clothilde Degazeuze recognised that her own sartorial style was going to be the best advertisement for her business and dressed accordingly. As her countrymen said, she fitted her skin, and never looked less than one hundred per cent *chic*. That morning's mid-thigh-length number was spangled with parallel fringes of white crystal and jet, worn over sleek black silk stockings. Round her short blonde hair was tied a black bandeau supporting an improbably tall black ostrich feather. Long strings of jet beads swung from her neck. Her face was white, her eyes heavily kohled, and her lips a slash of red.

Some of her dumpier clients might have been daunted by her elegance. England breeds a kind of Home Counties woman with a low centre of gravity who, generally speaking, looks better on horseback. Since most of them are married to men of small intellect but large wallets, they made up a lot of Madame Clothilde of Mayfair's clientele, and they could be a little awestruck by the perfection of the couturier, and of her equally immaculate subordinates.

But such a problem did not, of course, arise that morning. Clothilde never contemplated going into competition with Twinks in the beauty stakes. She knew she'd lose.

Madame Clothilde and her subordinates twittered around, making much of the new arrival. Twinks was a great favourite in the showroom. In part, this was because she brought them more custom than any amount of advertisement could have achieved. Though Twinks herself would never have been so vulgar as to mention where she bought her clothes, somehow the word got out, at all of the Hunt Balls, Coronations or royal funerals she attended, that she had been dressed by Madame Clothilde of Mayfair.

This had a doubly commercial benefit for the couturier. Unattached young women at such events, dazzled by Twinks's elegance and her effect on men (unattached or otherwise), beat a path to the South Audley Street address.

And young men, who had fallen for Twinks like sets of skittles, accepting that their dreams could never be realised and settling for Home Counties women with low centres of gravity who, generally speaking, looked better on horseback, sent their wives to the same destination in the forlorn hope that the magic of Madame Clothilde's scissors might make them less dumpy and more like the Twinks of their husbands' imaginings.

So Blotto's sister was always welcome in South Audley Street.

But this particular morning, as the entire staff of the couturier gathered around her, Twinks said, 'It is not for me, Madame Clothilde.'

The encoded message was understood. At once the proprietress ordered her staff to look after the showroom, and led her customer to the basement, which was the venue for her more private transactions.

'So, who is the character?' asked Madame Clothilde.

'A beggar. A street entertainer.'

'*Ooh, la la!* And you will be playing the part yourself?'

'Tickey-Tockey.'

'*Formidable!* Is she *une jeune fille* or an old crone?'

'My own age. I do not wish to disguise . . . my looks.' A woman more egotistical or less confident than Twinks would have said, 'my natural beauty.'

'*Vraiment?* I will see what I can find.'

Every space on the room's walls, except for the door by which they'd entered, was filled with fitted cupboards. There was a large central table, a few gilded chairs and a selection of tall cheval glasses. Clearly Madame Clothilde knew the cupboard's contents as well as she knew her own face in the mirror. Within moments, she had assembled a selection of garments and shoes on the table.

'I think what we should concentrate on,' she announced, 'is *à la mode d'Eliza Doolittle.*'

Pygmalion having been mentioned so recently, Twinks knew precisely what she was talking about. 'As in the play by that ageing *enfant terrible*, George Bernard Shaw?'

'*Exactement.* Eliza Doolittle is a flower-seller.'

'Tickey-Tockey. My character, though, will be trying to collect money for her singing and dancing.'

'Singing and dancing – *sacrebleu!* I cannot imagine the opinionated Mr Shaw allowing those into one of his long-winded plays.'

'You are right, Madame Clothilde. It will never happen. The day we hear that *Pygmalion* has had songs and dances added to it, we will know that the entire world has gone to the bonkers-doctor.'

Both women chuckled at the incongruity of the idea.

'Anyway, with your character and Eliza Doolittle, *c'est la même chose,*' Madame Clothilde assured her. 'The look will work for both.' She picked up some skirts from the table. 'And I think it is important that both are respectable characters. *Mais évidemment*, you are poor, but your *ensemble* is not of rags. You wear *vêtements* which are old, *mais oui*, but they have been patched and darned many times. This skirt, I think, will be right for you.'

It was made of much-repaired blue flannel, and ankle-length.

'So far as the look goes,' said Twinks, 'it's absolutely the nun's nightie. But I think I need to show a smidgeonette more leg when I'm dancing.'

Madame Clothilde understood instantly. And produced a skirt of similar dilapidation, whose hem would reveal Twinks's wonderful pins. 'Now, above the waist, I think a *blouse*, perhaps with loose sleeves, so that they will swirl as you dance.' She unearthed a garment which matched the description. 'Also patched and frayed, *comme ça*.'

Twinks was already stripping down to her elegant silk underwear to try on her new ensemble.

'And, *peut-être*, on top of that, a kind of *boléro* ... ?'

'Nothing too tight round the arms – again for the dancing.'

'*Très bien*. This one, I think.' A loose jacket of dark red, whose velvet had been worn away in places. '*Et maintenant*, it is just the hat ...' She produced a battered black straw boater, which Twinks placed, jauntily askew, over her perfect blonde bob. 'And the shoes ...'

This proved a little more difficult. The pumps and Mary Janes that Twinks usually wore were not robust enough for the kind of dancing she had in mind. Eventually, they ended up with a very scuffed pair of Victorian button boots with good hard soles. To add the final touch, one of Madame Clothilde's elegant acolytes was summoned and instructed to nail metal strips to the underside of the boots. For the tap dancing.

'And now, the *moment critique* ... or the *décision critique* ... What will you wear on your legs? A poor street entertainer could not afford silk stockings. She would wear stockings of *laine* – wool, perhaps? Or, more likely, none at all ... ?'

Twinks was faced with a dilemma. Authenticity was what she was after, and she knew that Madame Clothilde was a stickler for consistent accuracy in her disguises. But Twinks was also fully aware of the value of her glorious legs. For them to be displayed in anything other than silk stockings would blunt the impact of two of her most valuable weapons.

A compromise was reached. In spite of Madame

Clothilde's reservations, it was agreed that Twinks's legs would be displayed in silk, but a couple of holes and visible darns in the material would show that she was wearing cast-offs or hand-me-downs.

Fully dressed now in the whole ensemble, with the distressed stockings and the tap-toed button boots, Twinks was keen to view the effect in one of the cheval glass mirrors, but Madame Clothilde had one more final touch to add. 'The *visage* . . . and the hands . . . they are too soft and clean. They belong to an *aristo* . . . not to someone who lives on the streets.'

The couturier rooted around in one of her cupboards and produced an array of small glass pots of the kind that might contain cold cream. 'We have a selection here,' she said, as she checked the labels. '"Sewers of Paris" . . . *non, merci*. The make-up, I should point out, reproduces not only the relevant look, but also the relevant *odeur*. And the Sewers of Paris . . .' She wrinkled her elegant nose and read on from other pots. '"Sewers of London" . . . *non* again. "Thames Mud" . . . *je ne crois pas* . . . "Tottenham Stables" . . . ? Not a ladylike *parfum*, I think. Ah.' She held up one of the pots in triumph. '"London Smoke"! This will be *parfait*.'

Twinks did not argue as Madame Clothilde's hand dipped into the unappealing sludge and started to apply it to her cheeks and hands. She made sure there was a line of black under each of her client's delicate fingernails. '*Ne t'inquiète pas!* This will wash off with a little bit of *savon* . . . how you say? Soap!'

The couturier stood back and took in her creation. She looked very pleased with what she had achieved. '*Voilà! C'est magnifique!* And now you may look in the mirror.'

Twinks surveyed herself in one of the basement's many cheval glasses. Yes, Madame Clothilde had done an excellent job. 'Larksissimo!' cried Twinks.

'Even your own mother would not recognise you.'

Having grown up in the same house as the Dowager

Duchess, who frequently *didn't* recognise her own children, Twinks felt she might have to qualify this, but then realised it didn't matter. So she said, 'You've potted the black there, Madame Clothilde! I wish my bro Blotters was around. I bet he wouldn't spot his old sis. Ooh, I've had a thoughtette!' she interrupted herself suddenly. 'Our chauffeur's waiting in the Lag outside. Let's call him in and find out if he can recognise the young mistress.'

'*Bonne idée!*' Madame Clothilde summoned one of her elegant acolytes to bring the chauffeur downstairs.

But when Corky Froggett walked into the basement room, he did not notice Twinks. All he saw was Madame Clothilde. He cried out, 'Yvette!' and they fell into each other's arms.

Twinks drove the Lagonda back alone to the Savoy.

So good was her disguise, she had considerable difficulty in persuading the staff in the hotel foyer that she was actually staying there. It was only after she had produced her passport from her sequinned reticule, and done a dauntingly realistic impression of her mother, that she was allowed to go up to her suite.

In which, she spent the afternoon rehearsing for her evening performance.

The people queuing for returns outside the Pocket Theatre half an hour before that evening's performance of *Light and Frothy* were used to buskers trying to separate them from their small change. There might be an ex-soldier, wearing his medals and playing a wheezy accordion, a couple of tap-dancing kids who shouldn't have been out so late on their own, or a soprano whose high notes had subsided at the same pace as her bosom.

But never had they been so well entertained as they were that night. Some of them even risked losing their places in the theatre queue to get closer to the phenomenon they were witnessing.

Despite the scruffiness of her appearance and the grubbiness of her face, the girl's talent shone through magnificently. Her voice was fine and pure, her dance steps delicate and unfaltering. More than one of the makeshift audience expressed the opinion that, 'if the cast of *Light and Frothy* are half as good as this young woman, we're in for a corking evening!' The small battered basket the girl had left out for donations already gleamed with gold sovereigns.

It was just as the entertainer was about to sing her song, 'Kensington Cavalcade', that a short man wearing a black overcoat and black beret joined the fascinated throng.

Twinks transformed to full tear-jerking mode, as she went into her number:

'I sing on the street corner,
Come the sunshine or the rain,
And I watch the varied fauna
Who come strolling down the lane.
I see each lord and lady,
See the top hats on each head,
And, because my life's so shady,
I wish I was them instead.

'With my nose against their winders,
When my only source of heat
Is the chestnut-seller's cinders,
I feel sad and incomplete.
But the rich, so fine and free,
Will never notice me . . .
In their Kensington Cavalcade.
I try not to be dismayed
By all the wealth that is displayed . . .
In their Kensington Cavalcade.

'I sing my songs for pennies,
Just enough to buy some bread.
And all I hope for then is
A bit of pavement for my bed.
Oh, my clothes are rags and tatters,
Which I've had to darn and mend.
And, as the cold rain splatters,
Only poverty's my friend.

'With my nose against their winders,
When my only source of heat
Is the chestnut-seller's cinders,
I feel sad—'

'Stop!' cried the short man in black, interrupting her second chorus. 'Tell me, *ma petite*, where did you learn to sing like this?'

'Oh, lawks, guv'nor,' came a reply in Cockney, born rather closer to Bow Bells than the Ball's Pond Road. 'Ah started aht singin' in the church kwah, then Ah done singin' rahnd the pubs wiv the Sally Army.'

'But you did not 'ave any professional training?'

'Lord bless you, sir! When's a poor girl like me goin' to be trained to anything uvver than scrubbin' a doorstep?'

'What about your dancing? Is that self-taught, as well?'

'Well, ah never 'ad no dancin' teacher, if that's what you mean, no. Dancin' teachers ain't for the likes of me. Toffs 'ave dancin' teachers. People like me don't take dancin' classes. We take anything that ain't nailed dahn!' This last was accompanied by a throaty Cockney chuckle.

'But your dancing, it is *merveilleux*!'

'I dunno what that means, guv'nor, but if it's a compliment, fank you kindly, good sir.' And she dropped a neat curtsey.

'So, 'ow do you learn to dance like that?'

'Ain't got a clue, mate. I just listen to the music, and that, like, tells me what to do with my arms and legs.' The

Dowager Duchess, who had spent a small fortune on dancing teachers to develop her daughter's natural talent, would not have been pleased if she had heard this answer.

'And your *chanson* ... your song? Oo write this wonderful song?'

'Ah did, mister.'

'It is not possible. No girl can write a song like that.'

'Well, this girl did!' She was about to add, 'Wrote the bloomin' thing this afternoon.' Which would have been the truth. But caution prevailed. To admit how recent the song's composition had been might have raised suspicions about her serendipitous appearance outside the Pocket Theatre. So, instead, she said, 'I bin singin' it for years.'

'But the tune? Did you write the tune as well?'

''Course I did, matey.'

'*C'est incroyable*. That tune is as good as anything by Everard Stoop.'

'Don't know oo yer talkin' abaht, guv'nor, but that song – words, music, the whole rombooley – was all done wiv me own fair 'and. So, stuff that in yer pipe and smoke it!'

The man in black was amazed, dumbfounded for a moment. Then he said, '*Ma chérie*, you 'ave wonderful raw talent.'

'Oy, watch it, mate! Ah ain't raw. Not 'alf-baked neither, come to that. Done to a turn, Ah am. Ah don't know, there's you complimentin' me one moment, next you're bloody insultin' me.'

'No offence was meant, my dear young lady. And I cannot go on calling you "my dear young lady". Please, what is your name?'

Fortunately, Twinks had given some thought to the likelihood of this question arising. 'Florrie Coster,' she replied demurely.

'Florrie Coster ...' Pierre Labouze tried the name on his tongue. 'It is perhaps more a name for the Music Hall than Intimate Revue, but *n'importe*. It can be changed. Everything can be changed. *Bien, très bien*.'

The impresario extracted a card from his coat pocket and scribbled an address on it. 'Come to this place tomorrow morning, at nine o'clock sharp! And I will transform you into the biggest star the world has ever seen!'

As she walked back to the Savoy, to face more disbelief from the staff at Reception, Twinks thought to herself that her plan had gone rather well.

10

Threats of Matrimony

It wasn't at that moment much fun being Giles 'Whiffler' Tortington. For a start, he had no idea where he was. Straight after his abduction from outside the Pocket Theatre, the two men who'd manhandled him into the black saloon had blindfolded him. He had then been driven a relatively short distance – which suggested he was still in London – to what he took to be a private house. Only once inside had his blindfold been removed.

He had found himself in a small apartment, all of whose windows had closed shutters on the outside. The room in which he was incarcerated had functional furniture and no pictures on the walls. A large radiator mitigated the spring-time chill.

The main door was double-locked, and if he had contemplated escape, the continual presence of his two abductors would have foiled such plans. His guards proved to be singularly uncommunicative, hardly exchanging more than a few words with each other, and certainly none with him. His enquiries as to where he was, and what was going to happen to him, might as well have remained unvoiced. They elicited no information. Nor did questions about who was imprisoning him, and why.

Whiffler was not physically mistreated, though the muscular bodies of his minders, and the open way they wore their revolvers, suggested that, if he did resort to fisticuffs, he wouldn't stand a chance. And the unchanging diet of ham sandwiches (without mustard, for God's sake!) made him long for the nursery food at the Gren. He also missed his regular hauntings of London's stage doors. Above all, he missed Frou-Frou Gavotte.

Like many prisoners before him, he began to lose track of time. The shutters on the windows prevented him from seeing the outside light change, and, perhaps with a view to disorienting him further, the two men in black had confiscated his pocket watch. There was a reasonably comfortable bed, but whether he found the welcome oblivion of sleep in the daytime or night-time, he had no means of knowing.

Perhaps fortunately, he did not know about the hundred-thousand-pound ransom demanded for his safe return to his former life. Nor the fact that that deadline had long since passed, without any of the threatened consequences.

Then, suddenly – who could say how many days into his incarceration – someone new was admitted into the apartment.

The man wore the face of a pugilist, who had gone a few hundred rounds too many. He had cauliflower ears, and his nose shared qualities with a cauliflower too. But he was smartly dressed in a suit of sober black. And at his throat was the white band of a dog collar.

'Good morning, Mr Tortington,' he said in a voice of sonorous profundity. 'I have come to discuss the arrangements for your wedding.'

The Earl of Hartlepool had three reasons for telling his chauffeur to get the ageing Rolls-Royce out of the Little Tickling garages and drive him to London.

First, he was anxious about running out of matchsticks for his model, and his trusted supplier was a pipe-maker in an arcade off Jermyn Street.

Second, he wanted to attend a meeting of EGGS (The Eradication of Ghastly Guns Society).

And third, in the continuing absence of his son, he was more than ever determined to marry Twinks.

The same evening that his sister was entertaining the queues outside the Pocket Theatre, Blotto had spent at the Gren, meeting a few of his old muffin-toasters and generally putting the world to rights. He had staggered back to the Savoy and was trying to work out why the walls of his suite's bedroom were rotating around him . . . when the telephone rang.

The cowed voice of the flunkey from Reception forewarned him that the call with which he was about to be connected came from his mother. The Dowager Duchess did not like using the telephone. She was of the view that, if she spoke loudly enough, people should be able to hear her without any mechanical intervention. The result of this was that, on the rare occasions when she did use the instrument, she spoke even louder.

'Blotto,' she thundered. 'I bet, by this time of the evening, you're drunk.'

'Oh, I wouldn't say that, Mater. Maybe slightly wobbulated, but not—'

'Don't try that line with me, boy. I've known when you're lying since you were in your sailor suit.'

'Toad-in-the-hole, Mater!'

'Blotto, I'm telephoning to tell you you're giving me luncheon tomorrow.'

'Luncheon? At Tawcester Towers?'

'No, you idiot boy.'

'In London?'

'Of course in London! You're staying at the Savoy.'

'How d'you know that, Mater?' Blotto was totally snickered by her omniscience. 'Have you taken up mind-reading in your old age?'

'Don't need to do that, you voidbrain. I'm telephoning you at the Savoy, aren't I?'

'Yes.'

'So, the fact that you're answering from the Savoy suggests that's where you are.'

Surprised, Blotto could not but admit, 'Yes, I suppose it spoffing well does.'

'There's no need to use the language of the barracks, Blotto.'

'Sorry, Mater.'

He was seriously worried. The Dowager Duchess clung to her ancestral home like a limpet to the rock which her facial features so thoroughly resembled. Only something on the scale of a Coronation would detach her from the fastness of Tawcester Towers. And the fact that she was coming up to London specifically to see her son boded ill for him.

Blotto didn't have to wait long to find out the nature of the latest threat to his sunny equilibrium. 'The luncheon table tomorrow will be for four,' his mother boomed.

'You, me, Twinks and who?' he asked. Then, trying to remember what his English beak at Eton had taught him, he tried, 'Whom?'

'Your sister will not be involved,' said the Dowager Duchess ominously. 'One of your guests will be the Countess of Lytham St Annes.'

'Tickey-Tockey,' came the vague response from Blotto, to whom the name meant nothing.

'And the other will be her daughter, Araminta fffrench-Wyndeau.'

Broken biscuits, Blotto murmured inwardly. Though, having been told off so forcibly for a 'spoffing', he wasn't about to use such language out loud to his mother.

'I thought,' he said in a wavering voice, 'that I wasn't going to meet the filly till the Hunt Ball.'

'The previous schedule has been moved forward,' the Dowager Duchess responded. 'The Countess and I have discussed the matter. We both feel it would be convenient to get the ceremony out of the way before the next hunting season starts. Can't be faffing around with weddings when one should be focusing on foxes. You and Araminta will therefore be getting married in September.'

Blotto felt as though the last sustaining guy-rope of his personality had just snapped in a tornado.

Immediately after this upsetting telephone conversation, he had gone straight across the landing to Twinks's suite. His sister was bound to have some fruity scheme to extricate him from the current gluepot.

But, when he knocked on the door, there was no reply. And when he went downstairs for a St Louis Steamhammer in the American Bar (which he needed after the traumatic exchange with his mother), the flunkeys on Reception told him that, though they had seen his sister leave earlier, she had not yet returned.

They didn't mention that, when she left the hotel, she'd been dressed up as a Cockney street entertainer.

The address Twinks had been given the night before was of an old Church Institute off Fulham Broadway, a squalid part of London to which her dainty aristocratic footsteps had never before been drawn. Had she been dressed in her normal street clothes, she would have attracted much attention, and quite possibly become a target for street thieves. In the guise of Florrie Coster, her presence elicited nothing more than a few whistles and catcalls from labourers on building sites.

It was clear when she entered the Church Institute, at eight forty-five precisely, that its current usage had nothing to do with religion. Even at that hour, from behind closed doors came the sounds of musicians and singers practising. The building had been converted to use as rehearsal rooms.

Pierre Labouze, still in his trademark black, still wearing his beret, was waiting impatiently in the hallway.

'Ah, Florrie, you 'ave arrived. I knew you would arrive.'

'How could you be so sure, matey?' The question was, of course, posed in perfect Cockney.

'Because I am Pierre Labouze. I am the greatest impresario in the world. I make careers in the theatre. Nobody ever refuses a summons from Pierre Labouze.'

'Cocky little blighter, aintcher?' said Florrie Coster.

'What you call "cockiness", *ma petite*, is simply being aware of my *valeur* . . . my value to the world.'

'If you fink that makes you sahnd any less cocky, you're barkin' up the wrong fundament, matey.'

'Right,' said the impresario, turning on his heel and ushering her into one of the rooms. 'Now we find out 'ow much talent you really 'ave.'

The floor was bare boards, blinds had been pulled down over the windows, and the wattage from the overhead bulbs was dingily low. In the corner, at a shabby upright piano, sat a man who looked as dilapidated as his surroundings.

'Émile,' barked Pierre Labouze. 'She will start with scales. Give me a C!'

The lugubrious pianist struck a lugubrious note, from which Twinks sang the scale perfectly. This was stale bread for her. The Dowager Duchess's insistence that her daughter should have all the accomplishments to qualify her on the marriage market would have turned a gerbil into a viable matrimonial prospect. Applying such specialised tutoring to someone with Twinks's natural gifts could not fail to produce a prodigy.

Pierre Labouze could not fault her on the scales, but he was a man whose greatest pleasure in life came from faulting people, so he moved on to a stiffer test. 'Of course,' he said, 'you cannot read music.' It wasn't even a question; it was an assumption.

'Well, strike a light, guv'nor,' said Florrie Coster. 'As it 'appens, Ah can.'

'But 'ow could someone like you, a piece of vermin brought up in the gutter, 'ow ever could you 'ave 'ad the opportunity to learn to read music?' (It was noticeable that, in this dialogue between French and Cockney, initial aitches had been completely eliminated.)

Twinks realised she had put herself in danger of blowing her cover, so she thought quickly before responding, 'Self-taught, old cock, that's me. 'Ad to make the time to learn the dots. Got up at four-firty every mornin', to get me seven little bruvvers aht a bed, cos there's just me to look after 'em, since the cholera took away our muvver and our Dad fell in the Thames. So, every morning I have to see me little bruvvers is dressed and fed wiv bread an drippin' – includin' little Tim wiv the gammy leg and the crutches.'

She feared she was straying rather into Dickens territory and did a bit of self-correction. 'Then, when Ah've got them to the Board School, ah go dahn Covent Garden to pick up any loose flahs what got dropped by the uvver sellers, and I get togevver a few bunches wot I can sell on the street ahtside St Pau's Church there.'

Getting dangerously close to George Bernard Shaw now, she realised, and steered off in another direction. 'And when I sold me flahs, and maybe got a few farvings in me basket for me singin' and dancin', like, then I nip in the church and read the 'im books in there. And I see the straight lines of the music wiv all the dots goin' up and dahn, and cos I know the tunes of all the 'imms wot I learned wiv the Sally Army, I can understand them dots.' She looked at Pierre Labouze with a winning smile. 'And at's 'ow I learnt to read music.'

The impresario was silent for a moment. Twinks worried that she might have slightly overegged the pudding. But then he threw his arms around her and, sobbing, announced, 'But that is so *triste*. It is a wonderful story! It is a story the newspapers will love when you become a great star!'

'Oh, I just tell the trufe, mister,' said Florrie Coster modestly. 'That's just 'ow life is when you've been dragged up in the gutter.'

'*C'est magnifique!* Such odds you 'ave overcome. And such natural talent!' He released her from his embrace and looked cannily into her eyes. 'All right, I believe 'ow you learned to read music, but the *chanson*, the song you sang outside the Pocket Theatre last night, the "Kensington Cavalcade", I cannot believe that you wrote that. Tell me the truth – where did you get the song from?'

'Like Ah said, Ah writ it.'

'*Vraiment?*'

'Absolutely bloody *vraiment*, wotever that means!'

He clearly didn't believe her. Not that that mattered too much. '*Eh bien*, let us now find out the extent of your dancing skills. Émile, play the mazurka!'

And so began a morning of frenetic singing and dancing at a level that Twinks had not before experienced. Pierre Labouze was a fiercely hard taskmaster. He had very high standards for his artistes, and he took great pleasure in berating them when those standards were not met. But he had a hard time with Twinks. Whatever song he demanded she sight-read, she sang perfectly. Whatever dance step he wished her to demonstrate, she executed in a manner which would have satisfied Diaghilev. By the end of the morning, Labouze was the one who was looking exhausted, and it was he who called for a break.

Twinks was far too well bred to sweat, but her exertions had left her in need of a little restorative nose-powdering. That aquiline feature duly powdered, it was on her return to the hall that she heard the voice of Pierre Labouze emanating from behind a half-closed door. It was evident that he was speaking on the telephone. Reminding herself that the whole purpose of her subterfuges had been to get close to the impresario and find out his connection with Whiffler Tortington, Twinks listened intently.

The first part of the overheard speech concerned her exceptional skills as a singer and dancer. The kind of girl whose head was easily turned might have listened to this eulogy with rapture, but for Twinks, who had grown up from the nursery knowing she was brilliant at everything, his praise was of no interest.

It was the direction in which the conversation moved on that riveted her attention.

'So,' Labouze was saying, 'she is *merveilleuse*! She will be a sensation in my next revue. Already I am planning a sequel to *Light and Frothy*, which will be called *Light As a Feather*. In that show I will launch Florrie Coster as the new Pierre Labouze discovery.

'But . . .' His voice took on a lower and more conspiratorial tone '. . . she will also be perfect for our . . . other purposes. We can make a lot of money from her. The right kind of buyer will pay way over the odds for someone of her talent and beauty.'

Twinks's exquisite brow wrinkled. Was the idea to sell her into white slavery? If so, they would soon find out the kind of Britannia's daughter they were up against.

More importantly, who was at the other end of the telephone line? Who was Labouze's co-conspirator?

That question was quickly answered. 'And I am sure, with your contacts, the right husband for her can be quickly found. Wouldn't you agree . . . Everard?'

11

She-Who-Must-Be-Obeyed

'To lose one parent may be regarded as a misfortune,' said Everard Stoop. 'To lose both would leave you an orphan.'

He was at his customary post at the Savoy American Bar, surrounded by his customary coterie, who let out their customary appreciative laughter at his latest witticism.

'Being a parent,' the celebrated wit continued, 'is giving hostages to Fortune. And who knows what ransom Fortune will ask for your children's return?'

This again was, to the coterie, Everard Stoop's funniest remark since his previous one.

'*In loco parentis*,' he went on, feeling he had not exhausted the subject, 'means "travelling by train with one's parents".' More sycophantic laughter. 'To be a parent is to give up—'

Everard Stoop rarely stopped in mid-aphorism. Certainly, none of his coterie would have dared to interrupt him, so, as on this occasion, he interrupted himself.

The reason for his depriving his audience of another leaden witticism was the arrival, supported by a stick on one side and the arm of her son Devereux Lyminster on the other, of the Dowager Duchess of Tawcester. They were passing through the American Bar on their way to the Grill Room. Leaving his tall stool, long tortoiseshell cigarette holder and Martini, Everard Stoop stepped towards them.

'Your Grace,' he said to the Dowager Duchess, 'how enchanting it is to see you again.'

She turned on the writer the look she reserved for Labrador puppies who had misbehaved on the carpet of the Blue Morning Room. 'And who are you?' she asked, with a *froideur* which immediately halved the ambient temperature of the American Bar.

'I am Everard Stoop, Your Grace.' He waited for a response of recognition. Receiving none, he went on, 'Composer. Pianist. Lyricist. Sketch writer. My show, *Light and Frothy*, is currently running – to reactions of audience ecstasy – at the Pocket Theatre.' Still getting nothing back from the North Face of the Dowager Duchess, he elaborated, 'You and I were introduced at a weekend party at the Marquess and Marchioness of Tolworth's country house, Brinkmans, where I had the honour of providing after-dinner entertainment at the piano.'

She looked him up and down, as if examining wallpaper discoloured by yet another failure of the Tawcester Towers plumbing. Then, with the crushing force of a sheet metal roller, the Dowager Duchess announced, 'I cannot be expected to recognise servants.'

With that, she and her son processed through to the Grill Room.

Araminta fffrench-Wyndeau was, in Blotto's view, as pretty as a picture. A very pale picture, it has to be said. Pale skin, pale eyes; a boddo could almost see through her, like a shrimp in a rock pool.

Not only as pretty, he soon discovered, but about as articulate as a picture too. No doubt she had at some point undergone the same kind of training regime in ladylike accomplishments as his sister. He felt sure Araminta could sew, tinkle away on the piano and point a toe in the ballroom with the best of them. But she seemed somehow to have missed out on the conversation classes.

Not that Blotto minded. He had little to say himself at that lunch in the Savoy, as a miasma of misery settled around his patrician head. He thought mournfully of Dippy Le Froom's fate. Marriage had curtailed his freedom as effectively as a life sentence in Dartmoor. Blotto's old muffin-toaster had been forbidden to frequent the Gren. He had been denied the consolation of Xavier's cooking, and condemned to a schedule of eating home-cooked meals at home. He had been forcibly separated from all that might be enjoyable, rather in the way that, as the school chaplain had explained to him, Adam and Eve had been cast out of Ealing.

Dippy's wife Poppy had brought about this ghastly reversal of fortunes for him. And the simpering breath-sapper, now sitting opposite at the Savoy, was preparing the same fate for Blotto. No wonder he had nothing to say.

Anyway, the silence of the younger generation couldn't have mattered less. Their seniors did not leave a single edgeways-sized gap for a word to be slipped into.

Next to hunting, kicking Labradors, and shouting at the Tawcester Towers domestics, the Dowager Duchess's favourite pastime was patronising her contemporaries. And that lunch at the Savoy with the Countess of Lytham St Annes gave her the perfect opportunity to flex her be-littling muscles. It would have been easy for her, anyway, but, given the fact that the person in the opposite corner was an American . . . well, it made shooting fish in a barrel look tricky.

'The wedding itself will presumably take place at Spatchcocks,' the Dowager Duchess boomed, not being of the constituency who believed one should talk quietly in restaurants, 'despite the house being of such vulgar modern construction?'

The Countess of Lytham St Annes bristled to the ends of her considerable moustache. Decades of mixing with the right sort of people had done nothing to dilute her American accent. 'I don't know how you can call it "modern", Evadne,' she riposted. 'Spatchcocks was built on land granted to the first Earl of Lytham St Annes by Henry VIII.'

'Oh yes, I remember, Agatha. Henry VIII did ennoble all kinds of riffraff, didn't he?'

'I can assure you that—'

'While, of course, Tawcester Towers was built on land granted by William the Conqueror.'

'Oh?' said the Countess, in a voice larded with sarcasm. 'And no doubt the Dukedom was bestowed on your family by Jesus Christ?'

'That is a rumour,' replied the Dowager Duchess evenly, 'that has never been disproved. And I would point out that the proper pronunciation is "Dukedom", not "Dookdom". Now, as to the date for the ceremony . . .'

'September, isn't it, Mater?' said Blotto miserably. 'Before the hunting season begins. You said the two of you had discussed it.'

The Countess of Lytham St Annes bridled. 'I can assure you no such discussion has taken place.'

'Don't be tiresome, Agatha,' said the Dowager Duchess. 'I have made the decision. I'm not having the Tawcester Towers hunting programme upset by something as trivial as a wedding. The ceremony will, in fact, take place on September the fourteenth.'

The Countess, now very much on her high horse, bridled again. 'Might it not be more appropriate, Evadne, for you to ask me, as the owner of Spatchcocks and the mother of the bride, what I would consider a suitable date?'

'No,' replied the Dowager Duchess. 'You know full well that, in the English aristocracy, a Duchess outranks a Countess. And, in any circumstances on God's earth, someone who has had the inestimable good fortune to be born British outranks an American. So, in this matter – or indeed any other – I make the decisions. And I have decided that the wedding between my son and your daughter will take place on September the fourteenth. Now, let's talk about the other personnel who will be involved. Blotto will need a best man. That will be his elder brother, the Duke.'

'Oh,' said her son, not a little dismayed. He had rarely exchanged more than a couple of civil words with his elder sibling. 'I'd rather have one of my old muffin-toasters from Eton. Whiffler Tortington would fit the pigeonhole – that's if we've found the poor old boddo by then. Or Dippy Le Froom . . . if his wife lets him out for the day, that is. Or—'

'Your best man,' said the Dowager Duchess, in the voice that had shaped the British Empire, 'will be your brother, the Duke.'

'Tickey-Tockey, Mater,' a subdued Blotto agreed.

'And as for the bridesmaids . . .'

'Ah, yes, I've had some thoughts on that, Evadne. Araminta has hordes of young cousins, lots of them living in the States who—'

'I must stop you there, Agatha. Although, as the mother of the bride, *you* cannot be excluded from the ceremony, I do not wish to have the occasion downgraded by the presence of other Americans.'

Anger made the Countess forget her current aristocratic status. She went straight back to her Texan roots, as she protested, 'Holy cow, Evadne, you can't—'

But she was silenced, as the Dowager Duchess juggernauted on. 'The bridesmaids will be the daughters of my son, the Duke.'

'What, all of them?' Blotto couldn't help asking. His brother Loofah's fame, in upper-class circles, rested chiefly on his inability to produce a male heir to take on the mantle of his Dukedom. Well aware of the duties that came with his position, the Duke continued regularly to impregnate his wife Sloggo. And she continued to produce daughters. Blotto had by now lost count of how many nieces he had.

'All of them,' the Dowager Duchess confirmed magisterially.

The Countess was almost lost for words. The only one she could come up with was 'But—'

'Duchess outranks Countess,' she was reminded by her superior. 'So, you will see to it, Agatha, that an announcement of the engagement – and the wedding date of September the fourteenth – will appear in the Court Circular of *The Times* next Monday.'

'Why should it not appear earlier, Evadne?'

'Because the right sort of people will be involved in house parties in the country on Friday, Saturday and Sunday. And nobody gives their full attention to a newspaper at a house party. They focus better on Mondays.'

'And what?' asked the Countess. 'Shall I put the same announcement in the *Daily Telegraph* next Monday as well?'

'No announcement will appear in the *Daily Telegraph*,' boomed the Dowager Duchess. 'We don't want servants reading about our affairs.'

The Countess of Lytham St Annes managed to get out another 'But—', before the Dowager Duchess went on, 'Needless to say, there will be financial details to be sorted out before the union takes place. I will brief my man of business, and rely on you to do the same, Agatha.'

'Of course, Evadne,' agreed the Countess, now completely vanquished.

'So, all that remains, to conclude the practical side of this very convivial luncheon . . .' (The Dowager Duchess, Blotto reckoned, had a different definition of the word 'convivial' from that in common currency.) '. . . is for us to drink a toast, in the Savoy's best champagne, to the happy couple!'

As the two old dinosaurs of the peerage raised their glasses, Blotto found himself also questioning the definition of the word 'happy'. Looking covertly across at the life sentence sitting opposite, he didn't think Araminta fffrench-Wyndeau looked very happy either. She was still as silent as the second and third fs in her surname.

* * *

It was as they were walking through the Savoy foyer after lunch that they were greeted by someone Blotto recognised. The tweed suit hanging loosely on the thin frame, the tufts of hair flying in all directions, even the hands still discoloured with dust and glue, left him in no doubt that the Earl of Hartlepool had arrived.

'Hello. Any news of Whiffler?' asked Blotto.

'Whiffler?'

'Your son. Giles.'

'Why should there be any news of him?'

'Well, he has been abducted, hasn't he?'

Finally, the Earl of Hartlepool's memory re-engaged. 'Oh yes, so he has. Do you know, I'd forgotten all about that?' Whatever his faults, oversentimentality about his only child could not be counted amongst them. He turned to the Dowager Duchess. 'Good afternoon, Evadne.'

'Cyril, how good to see you.' She had instantly forgotten the mother and daughter with whom she had just had lunch, making no attempt to effect introductions, and indeed, completely cutting them out of the conversation. Again, it was a matter of status. Though Araminta's mother was a Countess, and therefore of comparable rank, the Earl of Hartlepool was a man, and took precedence. Also, on the Dowager Duchess's scale of values, he did not suffer the appalling disqualification of being American.

What was also in his favour was the fact that she knew him to be extraordinarily rich. Which may have had a big part in prompting the reaction it did, when the Earl announced, 'I want to marry your daughter, Honoria.'

'Really, Cyril?' said the Dowager Duchess. 'What an excellent idea!'

She had been offered a once-and-for-all solution to the problem of the Tawcester Towers plumbing.

That evening it was again cocoa that they had sent up to Twinks's suite. Comfort was what they needed, but even the comfort of cocoa was inadequate in their current circumstances.

'Have we ever been in such a treacle tin?' asked Blotto mournfully. 'Both of us lined up to twiddle the old reef-knot at the same time. Come on, Twinks me old combine harvester, you're a whale on wriggling out of tight spots. Surely you can thread your way through this particular needle.'

'You're bong on the nose, Blotters. Usually I can bat back anything the stenchers of this life pelt me with. But, in this case . . .' Her voice descended to the same level of despondency as his. 'I'm up against the Mater.'

'Tough Gorgonzola,' said Blotto, and he meant it.

'And if the Mater's got her mind set on the idea of me becoming the Countess of Hartlepool, a stampeding herd of buffalo wouldn't make her change it.'

'No,' her brother agreed gloomily. 'Any buffalo worth the name would simply turn tail at the sight of her.' There was a sombre silence, before he went on, 'And she's equally determined to see me manacled to Araminta of the silent *f*s.'

'Desolation heaped on desolation,' murmured Twinks.

Now, though deficient in the intellect department, Blotto was as honourable as the day is long (or short, according to the time of year). The interior of his brain was as pure as the driven snow, showing no track-marks of anything as intrusive as a thought. And it had certainly never played host to an *unworthy* thought.

Until that moment . . . A little-used synapse inside his brain connected two equally underemployed neurons, and the unworthy thought was born.

Someone more used to entertaining unworthy thoughts would have kept quiet about it. Unworthy thoughts are not often voiced, without unwished-for consequences. But to Blotto, the arrival of one was so unprecedented that he immediately shared his unworthy thought with his sister.

'Just had a stirring amongst the grey cells, Twinks me old gravy boat.'

'Yes?'

'Well, my thoughtette was . . . the Earl of Hartlepool has lots of the old jingle-jangle, doesn't he?'

'Undoubtedly. But if you think that makes the old ammonite even mildly attractive to me, then—'

'Rein in the roans a moment, Twinks. Let me finish my round.' His sister was appropriately silent. 'So, the Earl's got the golden gravy trickling out of his ears . . . much more so than the Countess of Lytham St Annes?'

'Yes. Give that pony a rosette.'

Blotto continued, 'Which means more of the old spondulicks will come into the Lyminster coffers from your twiddling the reef-knot with the Earl of Hartlepool than will come from my twiddle with Araminta fffrench-Wyndeau?'

'Still yes.'

'So, your proposed marriage will bring in more than enough to sort out the Tawcester Towers plumbing?'

'Yet another yes.'

'Which means,' Blotto came triumphantly to his conclusion, 'if you got twiddled with the Earl of Hartlepool, the plumbing would be sorted – and there would not be any need for me to get twiddled with Araminta fffrench-Wyndeau!'

He knew, from the look on his sister's face, that he'd gone way beyond the barbed wire. Her eyes drilled through to the core of him and exposed what he now knew to have been an unworthy thought.

He tried, unsuccessfully, to make up the ground he'd lost. 'Sorry, Twinks me old rhubarb-forcer. Wrong words came out of the old tooth-trap. Meant to say that, to sort out the Tawcester Towers plumbing, only one of us needed to get married, and then was going to suggest that it should be me who made the ultimate sacrilege.'

'I think you'll find "sacrifice" is the word you're looking

for, Blotto,' said his sister coolly. She didn't berate him any further. She didn't need to. Blotto knew how far he'd gone outside the rule book and was appropriately chastened.

Deftly, Twinks changed the subject. 'The Earl of Hartlepool's plan, so far as I can ascertain from the Mater, is that he and I should get married as soon as possible. And that, as soon as possible after that, I should bear a son and heir to the Hartlepool title and estates . . .'

'Toad-in-the-hole!' said Blotto.

'. . . thus disinheriting Whiffler. Which would be an absolutely horracious thing to happen.'

'So, what are you going to do, Twinks?'

'I'm going to find Whiffler and rescue him!'

'But how, by Denzil, will you manage to do that?'

'I've already got the bloodhounds in full cry. I am certain that the person through whom I will track him down is Pierre Labouze.' And Twinks quickly brought her brother up to speed with the progress she had made in contacting the impresario.

Her previous gloom had melted away, like a cloud in the face of summer sun. 'Don't don your worry-boots, Blotters!' she announced. 'We'll find a way out of these gluepots! We'll see to it that Whiffler doesn't get disinherited!'

Blotto didn't think it was probably the moment to say that the one aim of Giles 'Whiffler' Tortington's life was to get himself disinherited.

12

Devious Plans

'There's no way round it, matey. It's goin' to happen. So you may as well get used to the idea.'

It was the second visit to Whiffler's place of incarceration from the clergyman whose face looked as if it had been tenderised with a mallet, and whose sonorous vowels had been born within the environs of Bow Bells.

'But I don't want to get married,' Whiffler complained. 'Or rather, I do want to get married, but I want to get married to the person I want to get married to.'

Through this tangled syntax, the clergyman – whose name, by the way, was the Revd Jeremiah Enge – got the young man's drift. 'Sorry, matey,' he said, unapologetically. 'You don't have any say in the matter.'

'But aren't I at least allowed to know the name of the poor greengage who I've got to twiddle the reef-knot with?'

'Not till after the ceremony,' said the Revd Enge.

'But that's inhuman,' Whiffler protested. 'It's the kind of thing that may happen in primitive countries that don't know any better, but we're in England, the spoffing cradle of freedom. Forced marriages just don't happen here.'

'No? Seem to happen every day with your lot. How much choice does the average toff have about who they end up spliced to? It's all arranged by the parents, like a deal on the bloomin' Stock Exchange.'

'It may look like that, but—'

'Doesn't just *look* like that, it *is* like that.'

'But what possible benefit can come from me being saddled with an unknown filly?'

'Quite a lot of benefit.'

'Financial benefit?'

'You betcher. Otherwise, my bosses wouldn't be goin' through this whole rigmarole, would they?'

'And who are your bosses?'

'Wouldn't you like to know?'

'When I was in bed last night,' said Whiffler, 'and the two gorillas who're meant to be guarding me thought I was asleep, I overheard them talking to each other.'

'Oh, yeah?'

'And they said a hundred-thousand-pound ransom was demanded for my safe return.'

'Possibly.'

'They said it hadn't been paid.'

'Maybe not.'

'Well, I can assure you it never will be paid. My Aged P's never been sentimental about me.'

'So?'

'So the financial benefits arising from my abduction are already a hundred thousand pounds down.'

'Yes. No worries, though. That was only, like, a punt. To see if they could get a bit of the old mazuma on account. That was never goin' to be where the real financial benefit come from.'

'Well, for the love of strawberries, can you tell me where the "real financial benefit" is going to come from?'

'Sorry, matey. No can do. Now, about this weddin' of yours ... As you probably pieced together, I will be the one actually conductin' the service. And it has long been the custom that the officiatin' minister has a few words with the engaged couple, explain' to them the meanin' of marriage, the importance of the, like, commitment what they're takin' on.'

'Yes, me old boot-brush, but there's one thing I'm sure you've noticed . . . ?

'What's that then?'

'You talk about the engaged *couple*, but it can't have escaped your attention that, apart from you, there is only one other boddo in this room.'

'I had noticed that, yes,' said the Revd Enge, with some dignity.

'Well, shouldn't you be spouting out your little homilies to my unknown fiancée, as well?'

'I will speak to the young lady separately,' came the imperturbable reply. 'Now, marriage is an honourable estate, instituted by God, signifying the mystical union that is betwixt Christ and his Church. It is not by any to be entered into unadvisedly or lightly . . .'

As the Revd Enge droned on, Whiffler could have been back at Eton, listening to the school chaplain. And, as he had done then, he completely tuned out the religious burble and returned to his own thoughts.

But his own thoughts weren't very cheering ones.

'A pretty girl,' said Everard Stoop, in his customary clipped diction, 'is like a tune.' He looked appraisingly at Florrie Coster. 'And beauty, of course, is in the eye of the cigarette holder.'

He had never been a man to worry about using his aphorisms more than once (maybe in the hope that they might, by constant repetition, one day become funny). Anyway, he was completely unaware that Twinks had heard the line before. He was unaware that he had ever seen Twinks before.

She had been worried to find him with Pierre Labouze in the rehearsal room when she arrived, sharp at nine, the following morning. Surely, he would recognise her?

But no. Context is everything, and Everard Stoop had no reason to associate the glacially aristocratic Honoria Lyminster he had encountered in the American Bar at the Savoy with the grubby Cockney specimen called Florrie Coster, with whom he was being presented that morning in Fulham.

'Florrie,' said Pierre Labouze, 'I 'ave been telling Monsieur Stoop a great deal about you.'

'Oh, yeah?'

'And 'e would particularly like to 'ear your song.'

'Which song's 'at then?'

'The one I 'eard you singing outside the Pocket Theatre.'

'Oh, "Kensington Cavalcade".'

'*Voilà*. Do you have the sheet music for it? Émile will accompany you.'

'Nah. Ain't got no dots written down. All in me head. But don't fret yerself. I can sing it unaccompanied, like I did then. Yer ready?'

'*Oui*,' said Pierre Labouze.

And Twinks, in her guise as Florrie Coster, launched into a note-perfect rendition of 'Kensington Cavalcade'.

At the end, Pierre Labouze could not prevent himself from applauding. Everard Stoop, by contrast, did not move a limb. There was a sour expression on his thin face, as he said, 'And you claim to have written this song yourself?'

''Course Ah done, guv'nor. What, you fink Ah bloomin' nicked it from someone else?'

'That is exactly what I'm thinking.'

'Well, Ah wrote it, all wiv me own fair hand. An' 'at's the trufe, pure and simple.'

'The truth,' said Everard Stoop, 'is rarely pure and often extremely complicated.'

'But you have to admit she is good, she has the talent, *non*?' urged Pierre Labouze.

'The girl has a certain naïve competence, I agree. But if she wrote that song, then I'm the Emperor of China.' Clearly worried that it was rather better than anything he had ever written, he turned again to Twinks. 'Tell me, who wrote it really? Was it Nurl Card?'

'No, it was not Noël Coward,' she responded in her own icy voice, but before they could notice the lapse, went on, as Florrie, ''Ow many times do Ah 'ave to tell yer, Ah wrote the bloomin' fing mahself! And 'at's the trufe!'

'Truth,' observed Everard Stoop, 'is stranger than lots of things people make up.'

'Are you suggestin' Ah'm makin' fings up?'

'To make one suggestion may be regarded as a misfortune; to make—'

'Never mind this,' said Pierre Labouze. 'Her dancing, her singing, it is *magnifique, n'est-ce pas*?'

'Yes, yes,' Everard Stoop responded testily. He never liked being interrupted in mid *bon mot*.

'A couple of years in my revues on the West End stage, and then, for our purposes, she will be *parfait, non*?'

'She certainly has the potential,' the writer conceded.

'So, it is just down to you, Everard, to use your contacts in the right places . . .'

'Yes, I know, I know. You can rely on me. I will find the right place for her.' He spoke snappishly, still feeling upstaged by the excellence of 'Kensington Cavalcade'.

As Honoria Lyminster, Twinks was getting extremely annoyed by being referred to like a commodity. And she reckoned Florrie Coster wouldn't be exactly chuffed by the treatment either. 'Could you tell me what the bloomin' heck you're on abaht? Yer may not 'ave noticed, but Ah am still 'ere, yer know.'

'It is not your business,' said Everard Stoop dismissively.

'If it concerns mah future, then it certainly is mah flamin' business!'

'Oh, don't be tiresome, you little chit! Someone like you doesn't know the meaning of the word "business".'

'No?' Then Florrie Coster said, in her best Cockney, 'Business is the marriage of creativity and enterprise, whose offspring is profit.'

114

Everard Stoop looked very peeved. The girl wasn't only better at writing songs than he was, she also came up with better *bons mots*.

Blotto's morning started later than his sister's. Cosseted by his luxurious bed in the Savoy, he had just reached the toe-stretching part of his waking-up process. He was in a blissful haze of indecision, not yet sure whether he had the energy to shave, bathe, dress and go down to eat in the hotel restaurant, or whether he'd just have breakfast sent up to his suite, when the bedside telephone rang.

'Hello?' he said blearily into the receiver.

'This is Inspector Craig Dewar,' said the familiar voice.

'Good ticket.'

'And I wondered if you might have anything for me . . . ?'

'Ah. Tickey-Tockey.' There was a silence. 'What sort of thing?'

'Information. Didn't we agree that, if you got any information about the whereabouts of your friend, Giles Tortington, you would share it with me?'

'Ah. Yes. Beezer. On the same page now. Sorry, bit early. Brain's still in its jim-jams.'

There was another silence. 'So?' said the Inspector.

'So . . . what?'

'Have you got any information for me? Have you made any progress with your investigation?'

'Ah. Right. I read your semaphore, yes. Well, we haven't got far along the track, I'm afraid.'

'But you had dinner with Dolly Diller a couple of nights ago. Didn't you get any information from her?'

'No, don't think so. She seemed mostly interested in how much of the old mazuma I'd got – or how much I was likely to inherit.'

'Nothing else?'

'No change.'

'What about your sister? She's a lot brighter than – I

mean, she shares your skills as an investigator. Has she found out anything?'

'Not enough to fill a bee's belly-button, I'm afraid.'

'Nothing at all?'

'Well, she reckons the person who might have the key to unlock the wardrobe is that French boddo, Pierre Labouze.'

'Oh? But I bet she hasn't managed to make contact with him? Labouze doesn't talk to anyone.'

'That was the message we got on the bush telegraph, yes. But Twinks is as clever as a fox with a new brain, so she's managed to get him to talk to her.'

'Oh? How?'

And Blotto explained about his sister's transformation.

'So, she's with Pierre Labouze, as we speak, disguised as a singing-and-dancing flower-seller called Florrie Coster?'

'You're right on the right side of right there, Inspector.'

'Thank you very much, Mr Lyminster. Well, busy life we lead here at Scotland Yard.'

Blotto felt almost sure he heard a chuckle from someone who wasn't the Inspector at the other end of the line, but all he said was, 'What about you, me old trombone?'

'Sorry?'

'Have you got a juicy gobbet of information for me? Come on, uncage the ferrets.'

'I'm sorry, Mr Lyminster,' replied Inspector Craig Dewar formally, 'but I'm afraid it is not Scotland Yard policy to share details of our investigations with amateurs.'

It was the second time Blotto had received the same snub. He couldn't help feeling, after he'd put the telephone down, that when it came to the matter of sharing information, his relationship with the Inspector was a trifle one-sided.

The house occupied by Madame Clothilde of Mayfair contained four distinct areas. The ground floor was taken up by her salon, where wealthy women were measured and fitted for Hunt Balls, Coronations or royal funerals. On the floor above were the sewing rooms, where the couturier's designs, for dress-wear and theatrical costumes, were actually made. The basement, as Twinks had found out, was the centre of operations for Madame Clothilde's disguise and transformation activities. Then the two floors at the top of the house made up the couturier's private apartment.

And it was there that, since her reunion with Corky Froggett, Madame Clothilde – or Yvette – had spent most of her time.

Though neither participant was in the first flush of youth, their mutual ardour seemed to be undiminished, and their rekindled love made them both feel younger than ever.

'We will never part, *mon chéri,*' said Yvette. '*Jamais.*'

'"Jammy"?' the chauffeur echoed. 'Yes, I've always had things jammy.'

They both laughed. It was a private joke that they had shared in France.

'But, Corkee . . .' Her way of saying his name never failed to make the few hairs on the front of his shins tingle. 'Nothing now can stop us from being together for ever.'

'Nothing,' he said, 'except my duty.'

'Poof,' she said, as only a Frenchwoman can say 'poof'. 'That is what you always said during *la guerre*. But now *la guerre* is over. You have no duty to anyone now, Corkee, except to little *moi.*'

The chauffeur did not think it was the moment to tell her that all other loyalties in his life would have to give way to the loyalty he felt to the Lyminster family and, particularly, to his young master. He knew that you had to ration truth when in the company of women.

The first item on that morning's agenda for the Eradication of Ghastly Guns Society committee meeting was 'Apologies for Absence'. The first item on every English committee meeting's agenda is always 'Apologies for Absence'. Some outside observers have been known to comment that it said something about the national character. Would the members of any other nation start with apologies?

Such reflections did not trouble the brain of the Earl of Hartlepool. Nor did he have any interest in Item Two on the agenda, 'Minutes of the Last Meeting', because he hadn't attended the last meeting. He couldn't wait to get on to Item Three.

The meeting of EGGS was taking place in a private room at Biddles, a gentlemen's club of much starchier demeanour than the Gren. It was here that the Earl of Hartlepool, on his rare visits to the metropolis, invariably stayed.

Around the table sat the usual components of such committees. There were a couple of minor peers of the realm, a retired judge who didn't seem to realise he was no longer in court, a superannuated Colonel who had 'had a good war' (in the sense that he'd survived it) and two members of the Great and the Good, whose only activity was appearing on a variety of committees.

There was also a younger man, who was an idealist in the matter of banning guns. The rest of them treated his naïveté with tolerant cynicism. Youth must be indulged (he was in his late sixties).

A lot of other committees might also have featured female representatives. The country was crowded with women who, having bossed their families into submission, were on the lookout for other people to boss. And committees, supporting whatever cause (though most usually interference into the lives of the underprivileged), were a natural outlet for such frustrated energy.

The Chairman of the EGGS committee, however, was a profound misogynist. At home he submitted continuously to the will of his wife (who was on endless committees), and he did not want that situation to cast a cloud over his public life as well. So, he decreed that no women should be allowed on to the EGGS committee. And he prevented his ruling from being challenged by insisting that all meetings should be held at Biddles, an institution on to whose premises, since its founding, only one female had ever strayed. (This was still referred to by members muttering in corners as 'The Great Bishop and Actress Incident of 1889'.)

'Right,' said the Chairman. 'Item Three on your agenda. "Definition of the Word Gun".'

The Earl of Hartlepool beamed. It was at his instigation that this topic had made its way on to the agenda. And he had lobbied hard with the Chairman and Secretary to ensure that it got an early place in the listing. He knew how frequently items down towards the end failed to be discussed for lack of time.

'Maybe you'd like to start us on this one, Cyril,' said the Chairman.

'Well, yes, thank you. It is something to which I have given a lot of thought. The question we really have to ask is: Is "gun" an adequate word to describe all of the kind of weaponry which we wish to ban?'

'It's been perfectly adequate in the past,' asserted the retired judge.

'But does it cover the vast range of firearms which are now available, or have been available in the past? Cannon, mortar, flintlock, arquebus, musket, howitzer—'

'You can go on with your list as long as you like, Cyril,' said the retired judge testily. 'The fact is they are all guns. That is the word to describe them. You say the word "gun", and people in general know what you're talking about.'

'That maybe all right now, Cedric,' the Earl cautioned, 'but what about in the future?'

'What about in the bloody future?' demanded the retired judge.

'Cedric, I must ask you to moderate your language,' interposed the Chairman.

'Well, I apologise, but we're wasting our time on this item. There are far more important matters for discussion later in the agenda, and we won't get around to them if we keep maundering on about the definition of the word "gun".'

The Earl raised a polite hand. 'If I may just make a quick point, Mr Chairman . . .'

'Of course, Cyril. And then we must be moving on.'

'Certainly. I would like to draw the committee's attention to the dictionary definition of a "gun". It is – and I quote – "a tubular weapon from which projectiles are discharged, usually by explosion". Now I would suggest—'

'No one's arguing with your definition, Cyril.'

For this the retired judge received another reprimand from the Chair. 'Please allow Cyril to finish, Cedric.'

'Very well,' came the huffy response.

The Earl of Hartlepool beamed. He was really in his element. The only thing he enjoyed more than making his matchstick model was engaging in debate of this kind. 'I concede,' he said, 'Cedric's point about the word "gun" covering most existing firearms, but shouldn't we, as a responsible committee, be preparing ourselves for the possibility of other weapons being developed in the future? Weapons which perhaps aren't tubular, and which do not use explosions to discharge their projectiles. We don't want to be caught napping by the invention of something that does the work of a gun but doesn't come under the traditional definition of a gun. Now, I have prepared some discussion points, which I would like to circulate around the committee . . .'

The discussion of the definition of a gun continued for another three hours. At the end, it being lunchtime, the committee agreed (as committees always do) that a sub-committee should be appointed to consider the matter and come up with a report to be presented at the next meeting of the main committee. The other items which there had not been time to discuss (nearly all of them) would be added to the agenda for that day.

As he went through to the dining room to enjoy the

nursery food of a Biddles lunch, the Earl of Hartlepool felt the satisfaction that can only come from a good morning's work. And the glow that achievement brought to him was enhanced by the thought of his forthcoming wedding.

Twinks apparently preoccupied with Pierre Labouze that day, her brother felt at a loose end. He knew he was faced with two major problems. One was finding Whiffler, the other somehow getting out of his virtual engagement to Araminta fffrench-Wyndeau.

His sister was possibly making progress on the first, but he could see no escape from the life sentence represented by the second. Blotto felt deeply frustrated, unable to move in any direction.

Then he had a cheering thought of something he could do. He rang the stage door of the Pocket Theatre and left a message, asking whether Dolly Diller could join him for dinner after the show.

He was surprised, though not alarmed, that he didn't get a message back from her. He decided not to worry, and that he would pick her up after the performance.

So, after the Savoy concierge had organised him a ticket for the hottest show in London, he went to see *Light and Frothy* again. He was struck again that, though Frou-Frou Gavotte was pretty enough, Dolly Diller was the real bell-buzzer of the two. He felt excited by the prospect of the evening ahead.

But, as he waited outside with the other Stage-Door Johnnies (of whose clan he still did not think of himself as a member), he was astonished that, when Dolly Diller emerged, she cut him stone dead.

She looked through him like a shop window, strode past in her white fur, and got into a waiting black saloon with tinted glass.

Blotto could not begin to imagine what he had done wrong.

13

A Nice Little Business

'Maybe you can explain it to me, Twinks me old banana-skin,' said Blotto. 'I mean, I know women are strange fish, and liable to change their minds at the drop of an earring, but why should a breathsapper like Dolly Diller be decorating me old visage with lipstick one day, and not recognising me forty-eight hours later?'

'Is it possible, that when you last shared nosebags here, you said something which put lumps in her custard?' After their busy days (well, Twinks's busy day, anyway), they were consoling themselves with late-night steaks in the Savoy Grill. Twinks was now out of her Florrie Coster uniform, and of course dressed in something shimmeringly gorgeous.

Blotto searched the contents of his brain. It didn't take long. 'Can't think of anything. We parted as harmonious as two swallows on a telegraph wire.'

'What, you saw the young thimble to a cab?'

'No, she had her own "special taxi service".'

'And what's that when it's got its spats on?'

'A black saloon with tinted glass in the windows.'

'Doesn't that muster the old memory?'

His noble brow furrowed. 'Sorry? Not on the same page.'

'Where have you seen a similar vehicle?' Twinks prompted.

'Ah.' Recollection dawned. 'It was just like the one that picked her up from the Pocket Theatre tonight, now I bring the brain to bear on it.'

'And before that?'

'Before what?'

Twinks, not for the first time with her brother, gave up the subtle approach. 'And also,' she suggested, 'just like the one in which Whiffler was abducted?'

Blotto's jaw dropped like a trapdoor in a farce. 'Great Wilberforce, yes! I hadn't thought of that! Do you think there might be some connection, Twinks me old apple core?'

'I think there could be, Blotters. You know, the deeper we get into this case, the iffier the Stilton becomes.'

There was a silence. Blotto didn't say anything. He knew better than to interrupt when the delicate cogs of his sister's brainbox were whirring.

'I keep thinking,' Twinks pronounced, 'that it's all tied up with white slavery.'

'Good ticket,' said Blotto.

'Do you know what white slavery is?'

'No,' he confessed. 'I mean, I know that slavery is what a lot of the Lyminster jingle-jangle used to come from. It's basically getting boddoes to work for nothing. And I never quite know why people get so puce around the gills about that. It worked perfectly well during the feudal system.' Blotto shared his mother's view that the ending of the feudal system was a retrograde step for human civilisation. For families like the Lyminsters, it had worked perfectly. 'So, I know what "slavery" means. Not sure about the "white" bit.'

'White slavery concerns women.'

'Oh? Well, nothing wrong with that. I'm not against this spoffing suffragette business. I'm all for equality. So far as I'm concerned, women should have exactly the same rights to be slaves as men.'

Twinks wasn't interested in her brother's liberal

123

credentials. She went on, 'White slavery is the trafficking of women for immoral purposes.'

'Ah.' Blotto nodded sagely. 'And what does that mean?'

His sister leant across the table in the Savoy Grill Room. And explained it to him.

Blotto turned the colour of his rare steak. 'Well, I'll be battered like a pudding! What kind of stencher would do a thing like that?'

'I'm not sure, but I think Pierre Labouze and Everard Stoop have got their grubby hands in the cake mixture. Anyway, I'm about to find out more. I have a snitch.'

'Oh, bad luck, old girl. Want to use my snot-rag?' And he offered it across the table.

'No, Blotters. I used the word "snitch" in the sense of an informant.'

'Ah.'

'Someone who is prepared to lift the dustbin lid on what's been going on.'

'And why would your informant be prepared to uncage the ferrets? Out of the goodness of his or her heart?'

'Of course not, Blotters. Don't be such a voidbrain. He's doing it for money. In most areas of life, bro, a bit of the old jingle-jangle usually does the business.' She looked up across the room. 'Ah, and here he comes, right on cue.'

The maître d' had stepped across to deny entrance to the shabby figure, but, at a gesture from Twinks, he backed away. The newcomer wore a faded raincoat and a flat cap, neither of which he showed any intention of removing.

'Thank you so much for coming,' said Twinks, offering him an empty seat. 'This is my brother Blotto.' Clearly it was going to be an informal chat. Otherwise she would have introduced him as 'Devereux Lyminster'. 'Blotto, this is Émile.'

Since the scruffy figure had been allowed to enter by the maître d', he now got the full Savoy treatment. A waiter immediately hovered at his shoulder, proffering a menu.

'Would you like to order something?' asked Twinks.

'I'm a musician,' said Émile. 'Get me a bottle of Scotch.'

She nodded at the waiter, sanctioning him to do as instructed. Nothing was said until the bottle arrived. Ignoring the glass that had been provided, the pianist pulled out the cork and took a long swig from the bottle. He sighed with satisfaction.

'So . . .' Émile seemed to take in Twinks fully for the first time. 'You're not a real Cockney sparrer, are you?'

'You noticed?'

'Didn't notice back in Fulham. Seeing you here in that get-up . . . well, I'd have to be blind not to.'

'And you don't have any problem about sluicing the slime on Pierre Labouze?'

'Certainly not. When I consider the pittance he pays me as a rehearsal pianist . . . huh. No, I don't have any loyalty there.'

'And you'll keep quiet about the fact that I'm not really Florrie Coster?'

The pianist's lower lip jutted forward thoughtfully. 'Not so sure about that. Might do it . . . for a consideration.'

Twinks opened her sequinned reticule, extracted something and slid it across the table. Recognising a ten-pound note when he saw one, Émile immediately stowed it away in his grubby raincoat pocket. 'You're you, ma'am, and Florrie Coster's Florrie Coster. No similarity at all between the two.'

'Thank you. So, decant the haricots. What is the dastardly plot that Pierre Labouze and Everard Stoop are hatching? Is it something to do with white slavery?'

The pianist chuckled. 'You're way off the mark there.'

'But it is something to do with making money out of women?'

'Nearer the bull with that, yes. I don't know if you read the popular press, ma'am . . . ?'

'I have been known to,' said Twinks, sounding uncannily like her mother.

'Well, you may have seen reports of liaisons which

might come under the heading of "Prince and Showgirl Romances".'

'I have encountered such tittle-tattle.'

'Well, there you have it!'

'There I have what, Émile?'

'There you have what Pierre and Everard are getting up to.'

'What are you cluntering on about?' asked Blotto.

And even Twinks's finely tuned brain was confused. 'Could you provide a little further elucidation, please, Émile?'

'Well, look, I don't know who came up with the idea, but you are aware that Pierre Labouze makes his money from putting on revues?'

'Yes, we're fully aware of that,' said Twinks, feeling that Émile was rather slow in providing her money's worth. 'Don't teach your grandmother how to behave at a Coronation.'

'All right.' The informant took a long draught of Scotch. 'And he keeps finding these new performers for his shows, girls who come from nothing that he turns into stars.'

'We know that too.'

'Well, although Pierre's had his successes, producing revues is a dodgy game. Couple of years back, he tried to get one of his shows going on Broadway and lost a packet. So, he's always on the lookout for other ways of making money. And this is where Everard Stoop comes in.'

'I'm still not with you,' said Twinks.

'Nor am I,' said Blotto, predictably enough.

'Well, Everard's got a kind of *entrée* with the aristocracy. He gets invited to lots of stately homes, you know, to like entertain the toffs after they've had their dinner, play a few songs, in-house cabaret, that kind of stuff.'

'Oh, I know what you mean,' said Blotto. 'The oikish sponge-worm actually tried to claim acquaintance with the Mater, said he'd been introduced to her at some weekend party at the Marquess and Marchioness of Tolworth's country house, Brinkmans.'

'I hope,' said Twinks, 'that our mother put him in his place.'

'She did,' said her brother, relishing the recollection. 'With three veg and gravy.'

Twinks watched Émile down another gulp of Scotch. 'You may continue,' she said.

'Right. Well, through Everard's aristocratic connections, he checks out single toffs who've either got lots of the old mazuma or stand to inherit it. Then they get invited to see Pierre Labouze's revues, where they—'

Twinks was ahead of him now and completed the sentence. 'Where they fall in love with the female stars of the shows.'

'Exactly, ma'am. Everard and Pierre've had quite a few successes.' He mentioned a couple of names of showgirls who'd made lucrative marriages into the aristocracy during the previous year.

'So, they set those up?'

'Certainly. Thriving little industry they've got going there.'

'But how do they make money out of it?'

'They draw up contracts with the girls. If the marriage actually happens, the girls agree to pay a percentage of the estate's total income every year.'

'In perpetuity?'

'In perpetuity, too right.'

'But don't some of the poor little pineapples object?' asked Twinks. 'Don't the girls resent having their marriages organised for them?'

'Not a bit of it. Most of them come from nowhere, never had any of the old spondulicks. And their lives in the world of revue are short. Soon they're too old to attract the men like they used to, and impresarios like Pierre Labouze are very quick to put them out to grass. So what choice would you make, ma'am? Scraping an existence back in the gutter? Or living high on the hog with some chinless toff, having servants doing everything for you, and your only duty being to produce the occasional sprog?'

Twinks liked to think that someone in her position would have more life-choices than that, but she could see Émile's point.

'But,' asked Blotto, 'don't some of what you call the "toffs" object to getting their reef-knots twiddled that way?'

'No, they don't! They think their toast's been buttered both sides. They're used to being in the company of women who behave like effigies in a church. Women out the theatre at least move about a bit.'

The image of Araminta fffrench-Wyndeau came to Blotto's inner eye. Pale, bloodless, as if carved from cold marble. She was very definitely in the effigy class. Whereas Dolly Diller . . .

Twinks pressed on with her information-gathering. 'And this . . . business of Labouze and Stoop's has been pongling along for some time, has it?'

'Oh yeah.' The pianist mentioned a couple of recent aristocrat-weds-showgirl stories which the gutter press had covered with salacious relish. 'Pierre and Everard organised both of those. They'll be on a nice percentage there.'

'And you don't think there's anything murdier going on in their business . . . anything criminal?'

Émile took another long swallow of whisky. He was nearly halfway down the bottle. 'I can't see it's criminal. All they're doing is, like, running a match-making service. A profession what's got a long history. Nothing illegal in that, is there?'

'Maybe not.' Twinks was still trying to find a connection between the Stoop/Labouze operation and the abduction of Whiffler Tortington by heavies in a black saloon.

Blotto also wanted an explanation of the snub that he had recently received. 'Have you come across a pretty little greengage called Dolly Diller?'

''Course I have. She's in *Light and Frothy*, isn't she?'

'Well, I was wondering whether she'd got the odd finger in these toff-marrying pies?'

'Howdja mean?'

'Is she being lined up to marry some aristocratic boddo, who's got the jingle-jangle spilling out of his lugs?' Blotto thought, if she was, that might explain her unwillingness to have anything more to do with him, as an impoverished younger son.

But he didn't get anything on the subject out of Émile. 'I wouldn't know, but in her case, I'd doubt it.' And the pianist spoke the words as if they closed the conversation.

'Why do you say you doubt it?' Blotto persisted.

Émile made no answer, taking another long swig from the Scotch bottle instead.

But Twinks wasn't finished with him yet. She still didn't feel she'd got all the information she'd paid for. 'Do you know if this pair of filchers, Stoop and Labouze, ever use force to get the marriages arranged?'

'I wouldn't know about that,' said Émile. He said it in a way that suggested, even if he did have any information on the subject, there was no way he was going to share it with them.

Twinks tried a few more questions, a few changes of approach, but achieved nothing. Émile's shutter had come down.

Eventually, she gave up and asked, 'Do you reckon I'm now being loaded down the barrel for something similar – you know, being married off?'

'No doubt about it. Well, if you're talking about yourself, your real self, I wouldn't know. But that's certainly what they'll be lining up for Florrie Coster. A couple of years starring in West End revues, then married off to a toff. That's the way their little business works.' And, once again, he upturned the whisky bottle.

* * *

Before she went to bed, Twinks thought about the moral implications of what Émile had told them. Everard Stoop and Pierre Labouze's enterprise was rather shabby, not the kind of thing people of breeding should involve themselves in, but, as the pianist had said, it wasn't illegal. Twinks couldn't get rid of the feeling, though, that there was something else, something darker, going on.

Before he went to bed, Blotto didn't think about anything. Which was par for the course.

14

A Mystery Man

The following morning, Blotto was woken by a banging on the door of his suite before he'd even got into his toe-stretching routine. 'It's me, Twinks,' came a voice from outside.

He mumbled a bleary 'Come in!', and his sister was instantly by his bedside. She was dressed in her full Florrie Coster get-up.

'What are you doing up before the dawn chorus has even started gargling?'

'I'm off to Fulham. Rehearsal again. With those two stenchers.'

'Stenchers?'

'Pierre Labouze and Everard Stoop. Surely you remember what we heard last night about their little games?'

Blotto said he did, though his memory had not really woken up yet.

'Anyway, Blotters, I'm going to see if I can find out more.'

'More about what?'

'About the connection between those two filchers and Whiffler's disappearance.'

'Oh, good ticket.'

'And I'm still as curious as a cat in a fruit-cage about why Émile clammed up when Dolly Diller's name was mentioned.'

'Did he?'

'Yes, of course he did.' She restrained herself from asking her brother whether he ever noticed anything. 'Anyway, I'll see you later, Blotters.'

'Tickey-Tockey.'

'And, whatever you do, don't go poking the proboscis off your own bat into the affairs of Dolly Diller.'

'No danger, Twinks me old midge-repellent.'

And Blotto went back to sleep.

For Twinks, that day's rehearsal was different. As well as Pierre Labouze and Everard Stoop, other actors and singers had been summoned to Fulham. No one had thought to mention the fact to her, but it was the first day of rehearsal for *Light As a Feather*, Labouze's follow-up revue to *Light and Frothy*. It was clear, once scripts had been handed round, that the show was going to be a star vehicle, written round one central performer. Obviously, it had been written by Everard Stoop long before Florrie Coster came on the scene, but in her the writer and impresario had found their star.

Twinks could sense, from mutterings from the other cast members, that the elevation of a newcomer, with no theatrical experience, was not popular. Over the ensuing weeks, that might present problems for her. Because, although she now knew from Émile (who blanked her out that morning, as if he'd never seen her before) about Pierre and Everard's little money-making scheme, she was determined to follow through on rehearsals for a while. Twinks's finely tuned antennae had detected that there was some darker criminal activity going on, and she wasn't about to give up the disguise of Florrie Coster until she had got to the bottom of it.

It also occurred to her that this was the third day she'd gone to Fulham in the same clothes, in which she had already performed two days' worth of vigorous dancing.

While that might have been par for the course for the real Florrie Coster (had she existed), this breach of hygiene did not sit comfortably with the daughter of the Dowager Duchess of Tawcester. Twinks made a mental note to pay a visit to Madame Clothilde of Mayfair to extend the range of Florrie Coster's wardrobe.

'Right, Émile,' shouted Pierre Labouze, 'could you just play us through the opening number, which, as I'm sure you'll all agree, is another *triomphe* for the wonderful Everard Stoop!'

Twinks's instant thought was: Bet it's not as good as 'Kensington Cavalcade'.

'An opening number,' said Everard Stoop, 'is almost invariably one.'

The cast of *Light As a Feather*, who had all been told that Everard Stoop was 'the wittiest man in London', laughed appropriately – and sycophantically.

'I will sing it through first,' he said. 'First impressions are what a dentist begins his morning with.' More sycophantic laughter. 'Émile, take it away!'

To tinkling accompaniment, Everard Stoop sang, in his thin tenor:

> 'When you've pulled up stumps
> And you're in the dumps
> And it looks like stormy weather,
> When your brain's confused
> And you're feeling used
> And you can't hold things together,
> When your lucky charm
> Just causes harm –
> Like your lucky sprig of heather . . .
> You must change your style –
> Just put on a smile
> And make life light as a feather.'

For a start, thought Twinks, it's virtually the same song

133

as the opener to *Light and Frothy*. And I was right, it's not nearly as good as 'Kensington Cavalcade'.

It was a thoughtful Blotto who went down to the Gren at lunchtime. He had a couple (or so) of drinks with some of his old muffin-toasters, and then went through with them to lunch, where a good few bottles of the club claret were put away.

But, though far from literally sober, Blotto was in a sober mood. The Gren just didn't feel the same without Dippy Le Froom and Whiffler Tortington. The one, he knew, was a victim of marriage. But what had Whiffler been a victim of? Blotto had to find out.

He couldn't get out of his head the response he'd received from the pianist Émile the night before, when he'd asked if Dolly Diller was being lined up to marry some rich aristocrat. 'In her case, I doubt it.'

It had been a strange answer, and one that implied there were secrets in the life of Dolly Diller.

Though he knew it was going against the advice Twinks had given him, Blotto was determined to find out what those secrets were.

After all, he reasoned with himself, Twinks isn't always right. (Though, actually, if he'd looked back over their shared past, he would have remembered that, in fact, she always was.)

Because it was the first day of rehearsal for *Light As a Feather*, in the afternoon the cast members had to be measured for their costumes. Once again, the design of these would be in the expert hands of Madame Clothilde. For most of the cast, this meant an encounter in Fulham with one of the couturier's immaculate subordinates, wielding a tape measure. For the show's star, it meant a taxi-ride to Mayfair for a private appointment with the designer herself.

This couldn't have suited Twinks better. It saved her making an appointment to arrange the expansion of Florrie Coster's wardrobe.

She was surprised, when she announced herself in the ground-floor salon, that Madame Clothilde was not there, and had to be summoned by intercom from her elegant living quarters at the top of the building.

When the couturier did appear, she was not quite her customary perfectly appointed self. While in no way scruffy, she did look only ninety-nine per cent glamorous. And for Madame Clothilde, one percentage point was a huge deficiency.

The man who followed sheepishly behind her, with one button of his chauffeur's uniform undone, looked positively dishevelled. Twinks was only slightly surprised to recognise Corky Froggett.

'Erm, good afternoon, milady,' he said awkwardly. 'I must go and polish the Lagonda.' And he scuttled out of the salon.

Neither Twinks nor Madame Clothilde made any mention of Corky's presence – or indeed absence. 'You did know that I had an appointment this afternoon?' asked Twinks.

'*Mais évidemment.*'

'It's for my *Light As a Feather* costumes.'

'*D'accord.* For such a consultation we would normally go to one of the rooms upstairs. Today we go to the basement.'

Twinks was glad that Madame Clothilde was treating the situation with appropriate seriousness.

'So . . . have Pierre Labouze or Everard Stoop seen through your disguise?'

'No.' Twinks dropped into Florrie Coster's Cockney. 'Them two fink Ah was dragged up in a gutter off the Balls Pond Road.'

'*Formidable!* And I am sure you are here because Florrie Coster needs a little variety in her *ensembles*?'

'You're as sharp as a needle that's cut its way through a haystack, Madame Clothilde.'

'Oh, please . . . I think we know each other well enough for you to call me "Clothilde".'

'Tickey-Tockey . . . Clothilde.'

'I had already considered the possibility, *chérie*, that your wardrobe might be in need of a little enhancement.' Madame Clothilde opened one of the many cupboards to reveal an array of suitably tattered and much-repaired garments. 'Take as many as you wish. You will be rehearsing with Pierre Labouze for a long time, I think?'

'Only for as long as it takes me to find out what the stencher's really up to. Then I'll be off out of that rehearsal room like a cheetah on spikes.'

'What are you talking about?'

Quickly, Twinks gave Madame Clothilde a summary of what she had been told by Émile the previous night.

'This does not surprise me. In France Pierre Labouze has a bad reputation for mismanaging his financial affairs: many debts, many bankruptcies. He is the sort of man who is always trying some new scheme for money-making.'

'Yes, but I think the filchers have got something else going on; something where the Stilton's even iffier.'

'Perhaps,' came the guarded response.

Twinks was instantly alert. 'Do you know something, Clothilde? Come on, uncage the ferrets!'

'It is just . . . I have designed many revues for Pierre Labouze . . .'

'I know.'

'So, I have seen a lot of things that go on backstage . . .'

'Fumaciously criminal things?'

'Not necessarily. Mostly things like this marrying-off of showgirls to aristocrats . . . morally dubious, perhaps, but not downright criminal . . . There is one of the soubrettes, however, of whom I have more serious suspicions . . .'

'Well, come on, Clothilde! Don't shuffle round the shrubbery. Who are you talking about?'

'You have met the showgirl called Dolly Diller?'

'You bet your elbow patches I have! My brother Blotto thinks she's the lark's larynx. Well, he did a couple of nights ago, when she was larding him with lipstick. Last night, though, she gave him the ice cream's elbow.'

'Did she? That is interesting. And the first night, when she was pleasant to him, what did she talk to him about?'

Twinks could answer this in some detail. She had made Blotto go through his entire conversation with Dolly Diller – or, at least, as much of it as he could remember. 'She seemed very interested in the Lyminster family history . . . in how much we were worth, how much Blotto himself was worth . . .'

Beneath her expertly applied make-up, Madame Clothilde turned pale. 'This is *très mauvais*,' she said. 'Not good.'

'Oh?'

'I think your brother is in great danger.'

'What? Why?'

'Have you heard of a man called Barmy Evans?'

'No. Who's he when he's got his spats on?'

'Barmy Evans is one of the most wicked villains in London.'

'Is he, by Denzil? But what's he got to do with Blotto?'

'Barmy Evans is the . . . what is the *mot juste*? He is the "protector" of Dolly Diller. He does not like it when other men get interested in Dolly Diller.'

'Oh?'

'In fact, he has killed every other man who has got interested in Dolly Diller.'

'Lawkins!' said Twinks. And she meant it.

Waiting outside the stage door of the Pocket Theatre had become rather familiar to Blotto. It still never occurred to him that he could be described as a Stage-Door Johnny, but he noticed there were fewer of them around before the show than there would be after. And, in the message he'd sent from the Savoy, he'd suggested having a quick word with Dolly Diller before that night's performance of *Light and Frothy*. Then they could breezily clear up why she'd given him the ice cream's elbow the previous night, and make arrangements about where they would dine after the show.

Blotto thought back to the first night he'd been to the Pocket Theatre, the night that Whiffler Tortington had been abducted.

And, even as he had the thought, the situation become even more familiar, as a black saloon with tinted windows drew up in front of the theatre. Two men in black overcoats, with black hats pulled down over their eyes, got out of the back. Anyone other than Blotto might have thought he was experiencing déjà vu, but he didn't know the expression, not having got that far in French at Eton.

The two men in black held the car door open, and Dolly Diller emerged, dressed once again in her white fox-fur coat.

As Blotto stepped forward to greet her, she pointed at him and said, 'That's the one Barmy wants to see.'

She continued on her way to the stage door. Blotto was so surprised that he didn't have time to resist, as the two men in black seized him, one taking each arm, and bundled him into the back of the car.

15

Muffin-Eaters Reunited!

Blotto was blindfolded, and his wrists were handcuffed behind his back, but he still reckoned he could have got away from his captors if he'd wanted to. He certainly could have done so if he'd had his cricket bat with him. Some instinct, however, kept him from making any attempt to escape.

He managed to convince himself that this was a matter of strategy. He, Devereux Lyminster, wasn't stupid enough to have fallen into the trap that had been prepared for him. No, no, he had willingly put himself into jeopardy, with a view to advancing his investigation into Whiffler's disappearance.

So, he waited to see where the men in black were taking him.

And, when his blindfold was finally removed, he realised just how percipient he had been.

Because, facing him, in an anonymous flat less than half an hour's drive from the Pocket Theatre, was Giles 'Whiffler' Tortington.

Splendissimo! thought Blotto, borrowing one of his sister's favourite expressions, I've ponged the partridge!

Out loud, he said, 'Spoffing good to see you, Whiffler me old Eccles cake!'

His old muffin-toaster gaped in surprise, unable to form

words. His instinct was to go forward and shake Blotto by the hand, but being chained to one end of a radiator made that difficult.

'You two may go,' said Blotto to the men in black, with a curtness which could only come from generations of inbreeding.

The two subordinates, with the automatic compliance to aristocratic instructions which also had a long history, retired from the room, closing the door behind them.

'Well, Whiffler,' said Blotto cheerfully, 'we're rolling on camomile lawns, aren't we?'

'In what way?' asked his old muffin-toaster.

'Great Wilberforce, I've found you, haven't I? I've been looking for you, and I've found you! I have completed my quest. My quest to locate Giles "Whiffler" Tortington has been completed. I feel like one of King Arthur's knights actually placing his stickies on the Holy Gruel.'

'Ye-es,' said Whiffler, not totally convinced.

'Oh, come on. There's nothing to go all bliss-bereft about. We only have to get out of this place, and life can continue on the straight track to Paradise Mountain.'

'Things aren't that jammy, Blotters. I've been here for days and days, trying to work out how to escape, and there isn't a cranny for a woodlouse to crawl through.'

Blotto was in no mood to be disheartened. 'This place'll be as easy to get out of as a one-bush maze.'

'Oh yes? You appear not to have noticed that I am handcuffed to a radiator. You've got handcuffs on too. You'll have to get out of those before you start thinking of escaping.'

'No hitch there. Boddoes like me can always unlock handcuffs with a bent hairpin.'

'I haven't seen too many hairpins, bent or otherwise, in this fumacious swamp-hole.'

'Don't be dump-downed. Where's the carefree Whiffler with whom I used to toast muffins at Eton?'

'Far from carefree. And so would you be, if you'd been in this clammy corner as long as I have. On a diet of ham sandwiches – without mustard!' Blotto winced at the idea of such cruel deprivation. 'And it's particularly vexing, since I haven't got a mouse-squeak of an idea why I've been locked up in here.'

'Oh, I might be able to uncage the ferrets on that one, Whiffler. I think Pierre Labouze and Everard Stoop are behind this little plot. You know who I mean?'

'Of course I do. The producer and writer of *Light and Frothy*.'

'Exactly. Give that pony a rosette! Well, they've got a rather devious wheeze on the wire, and that's why they've had you kidnapped. The juice of it is: they want to marry you to a showgirl!'

'But that's all I want, Blotters. I want to be married to a showgirl!'

Blotto hadn't considered this before, but Whiffler's words made him realise that there actually was some beef in it. 'Good ticket,' he agreed.

'The only slice of cheesecake I ask for in life is to be married to Frou-Frou Gavotte!'

'Yes, but suppose these stenchers are lining you up in the traps to be married to some other showgirl . . . ?'

'That would absolutely be the flea's armpit.'

'Well, don't let's don our worry-boots about it now, Whiffler me old pot-spurtle. First tick on the to-do is to get out of this place.'

'There is no way out of this place!'

'Oh, really, Whiffler! Don't put a damp sock in the trumpet. Where's the Tortington spirit that won the Battle of Bosworth Field?'

'Actually, the Tortingtons didn't win the Battle of Bosworth Field. We were on the other team – Yorkists: White Rose, don't you know?'

'Ah.' The Lyminsters had actually been Lancastrians – Red Rose, and therefore on the winning side. But Blotto didn't think it was the moment to revive old rivalries from 1485. Instead, he said, 'Come on, Whiffler! Gird up the sinew! We've only got two men in black to beat!'

'Make that three.'

They hadn't heard the door open, but both turned to see, in its frame, a third man in black.

16

A Political Criminal

Lurking behind the newcomer were the two guards, and also a man with a dog collar and the face of a boxer (canine or pugilistic, take your pick). Whiffler knew who this last was, though Blotto had never seen him before. The way the three of them stood left no doubt that the man in front was in charge. He was not tall, but very muscular, and he had the kind of large moustache which Joseph Stalin would go on to make popular (or unpopular, according to your point of view). Pockmarks made his face look as though it had been used as a rifle range.

'Hello,' he said. 'I'm Barmy Evans.' His voice was rough, but still had the slight singsong quality of the Welsh valleys where he had grown up.

Since neither Blotto nor Whiffler had heard his name before, it did not strike into their hearts the terror which it rightly should have done.

'Chain that one!'

The two men in black moved so quickly that Blotto hadn't time to stop them from chaining him by his handcuffs to the end of the radiator not occupied by Whiffler.

'The time has come,' Evans went on, stroking his luxuriant moustache, 'to decide what's going to happen to you two.'

'I think I may be a move ahead of you on the chessboard

here,' said Blotto, feeling rather proud of himself. Twinks had warned him off trying to pursue the investigation, and here he was, having wormed his way into the villains' lair. So, snubbins to her! 'I think I know, Mr Evans, your plans for my friend here, Giles "Whiffler" Tortington.'

'Oh, do you?'

'Yes, it's all part of a wocky scheme you've worked out with those four-faced filchers, Pierre Labouze and Everard Stoop.'

'Is it?'

'Bong on the nose it is. You're planning to marry Whiffler off to a showgirl, who'll then pay you murdy lumps of toadspawn a percentage of her new-found wealth.'

The looks exchanged by the two men in black and the dog-collared one showed Blotto that he was on the right track.

'Congratulations on your research,' said Barmy Evans drily. 'That's exactly what we're planning to do. That's why the Reverend Enge's here – to take Mr Tortington off to his wedding.'

Whiffler's red face took on tones of patriotic blue and white as he boldly protested. 'I'd rather die than twiddle the old reef-knot with someone I don't want to marry!'

Blotto recognised the moment when support for one of his old muffin-toasters was required. 'And I will lay my life on the line too, to foil your fumacious plots!' How he would do this, while handcuffed to a radiator, was not something he considered. Only cowards (or sensible people) would allow themselves to think like that, in the face of danger.

Whiffler continued, channelling the valiant spirit with which the Tortingtons had lost the Battle of Bosworth Field. 'The only person I am ever going to marry is Frou-Frou Gavotte!'

There was a shocked silence, before Barmy Evans said, 'Actually, it's Frou-Frou Gavotte we are going to marry you to.'

'Great galumphing goatherds!' said Whiffler.

'Toad-in-the-hole!' said Blotto.

'Release him,' said Barmy Evans.

One of the men in black moved forward with a key to detach the prisoner from the radiator.

'So, are you telling me, Mr Evans,' asked Whiffler, rubbing his wrists where the cuffs had chafed, 'that I was kidnapped outside the Pocket Theatre with the sole purpose of getting me married to Frou-Frou Gavotte?'

'Well, yes,' the criminal mastermind was forced to admit.

Giles 'Whiffler' Tortington stepped forward. 'May I shake you by the hand? You're a Grade A foundation stone.'

Awkwardly, Barmy Evans allowed his hand to be shaken.

'So, shall I take him to the church?' asked the Reverend Enge. 'Just like we planned?'

'Yes,' said his boss testily. 'Get them married as soon as possible.'

'Praise be to sausages!' said the ecstatic Whiffler.

'And there won't be any problem,' asked the Reverend Enge, 'with you signing a contract with us, agreeing to give ten per cent of your family income?'

'No problem at all,' said the ecstatic Whiffler.

'The Earl of Hartlepool's so loaded that it wouldn't be more than a fleabite to him,' observed Barmy Evans with a grim chuckle.

'So, everybody's rolling on camomile lawns,' said the ecstatic Whiffler.

Blotto didn't think the miscreants should be let off that easily. 'You may think you're very clever, Mr Evans, but in fact you have slightly plumped for the wrong plum here.'

'Oh yes?'

'You'll be on ten per cent of all Whiffler's jingle-jangle . . .'

'That is my understanding, yes.'

'. . . which you think will be ten per cent of all the income from the Little Tickling estate, when his Aged P shuffles off the old mortal . . .'

'Exactly.'

'But, in fact, you've been rather hoist with your own petunia.'

'Oh?'

'You see,' said Blotto, presenting his pay-off with great aplomb, 'Whiffler is planning to renounce the title, so he won't inherit anything!'

Funny, although he wasn't necessarily the most intellectually gifted denizen of the planet, Blotto could sometimes be surprisingly sensitive to the expressions on people's faces. And it took only one look at Whiffler's to tell him he'd said the wrong thing.

Blotto had heard the phrase 'a brow like thunder', but had never seen such a thing before the one which was now erupting on Barmy Evans's forehead, and echoing around the local mountaintops. 'Is this true?' the villain demanded.

'Well, erm . . . erm . . . erm . . .' was the total of the repartee that Whiffler could come up with.

'So, am I to take him off to get married?' asked the Reverend Enge.

'Certainly not! Tell me, Mr Tortington, is your mother still alive?'

'No, I'm afraid she tumbled off the trailer some years back.'

'And is it your intention, when your father dies, to renounce the Earldom?'

Whiffler, honest to the sloes of his Argyle golfing socks, could not deny that it was.

'Guns!' said Barmy Evans suddenly.

Clearly, it was an order his henchmen had heard before. Instantly, revolvers appeared in the hands of the two men in black. They materialised too for Barmy Evans, and even for the Reverend Enge.

146

Evans nodded to one of the guards. 'Take this specimen . . .' he gestured to Whiffler 'to the other room.'

'And shoot him?' the men in black suggested.

'No, you idiot! You're far too keen on shooting people. I heard you even tried to take a pot-shot at this same toff in the Pocket Theatre some days back.'

'It seemed a good opportunity. I thought—'

'You're not paid to think. You're paid to obey orders. I'm the one who decides who lives and who dies. Got that?'

The chastened man in black mumbled that, yes, he had got it. He gestured towards Whiffler. 'So, what do I do with this toff?'

'Manacle him!'

And, before Blotto had time to intervene, his protesting muffin-toaster had been dragged away to the next room.

'You,' Barmy Evans barked at the other man in black, 'get together some of the boys, and go and abduct the Earl of Hartlepool!' The man exited straight away.

'Rev,' Evans went on, to the battered clergyman. 'As soon as we've got the Earl, you marry him to Frou-Frou – right?'

'Right, boss. Do you want me to stay?'

'No. You go and help the boys abducting the Earl of Hartlepool. They're useless. I've never met anyone with less brainpower than they've got.'

Blotto, well aware of his own deficiencies in the intellectual department, didn't think it was the moment to contest this statement.

'Right-ho, boss.' The clergyman disappeared.

Barmy Evans stroked his moustache, as he took a long, assessing look at Blotto. 'Now,' he said, 'I have to decide what to do about you.'

'Well, sorry to put lumps in your custard, but I'm not worth marrying off to anyone. I'm the second son, you see, and—'

'I know all that,' Evans growled. 'You weren't abducted to get married.'

147

'Oh? Then why was I abducted?'

'You were abducted because you've been fingering my property. Dolly Diller. And I have a special way of dealing with people who finger my property.'

Broken biscuits, thought Blotto.

But he was only downcast for a moment. As ever, his sunny disposition quickly reasserted itself. He was unarmed, chained to a radiator, alone in a room with a homicidal career-criminal carrying a gun.

Those were the kind of odds Devereux Lyminster enjoyed. If only he'd had his cricket bat with him . . .

When she got back to the Savoy, Twinks tried ringing through to her brother's suite but got no reply. She called Reception and was told that Mr Lyminster's key was still hanging on the board there. And no, he had given no indication of where he would be spending the day.

Twinks was worried. Though she had given Blotto specific instructions not to do any investigating off his own bat, she knew his chivalric – not to say 'quixotic' – nature too well to have full confidence that he would have followed her advice. He was more than capable of having dived into another gluepot.

She crossed the landing and, extracting her skeleton keys from her sequinned reticule, had no difficulty in gaining access to her brother's suite. She did not need to go into the bedroom. Though she hadn't quite known what she was looking for, she found it on the desk in the sitting room: a Savoy notepad on the top page of which was written, in fountain pen, 'Detective Inspector Craig Dewar', and a telephone number.

Not even going back to her own suite to make the call, Twinks asked the hotel switchboard to connect her to the Inspector. 'Is that Scotland Yard?' she asked.

Her question was greeted by a raucous laugh from the

148

other end of the line. 'Is this Scotland Yard? Yes, of course it is, darlin'.'

'Could I speak to Detective Inspector Craig Dewar, please?'

'Detective Inspector Craig Dewar?' There was more laughter and shushing heard from the other end of the line, then a sober-sounding voice said, 'This is Detective Inspector Craig Dewar. Who am I speaking to?'

'My name is Honoria Lyminster.'

'Ah. I'm assuming you are the sister of Mr Devereux Lyminster?'

'You're bong on the nose there.'

'And are you calling me because your brother asked you to do so?'

'No, I'm calling because my brother seems to have disappeared.'

'When did you last see him?'

'This morning.'

'Well, I don't think we need be sending out the search parties yet, Miss Lyminster. I'm sure there are plenty of distractions in London to keep a young man away from his hotel for a few hours and—'

'I am calling you, Inspector, because I believe that my brother has been abducted.'

'Oh yes? And who might he have been abducted by?'

'Barmy Evans.'

'We'd better meet,' said Detective Inspector Craig Dewar tersely.

It was too late at night to telephone most people, but Twinks knew that she would instantly get through to Professor Erasmus Holofernes in his rooms at St Raphael's College, Oxford. He would by then have dined at High Table with his Senior Common Room colleagues and be back in his room, hard at research amidst the chaos of

149

papers and correspondence through which only he could find his way.

As anticipated, the Professor was delighted by her call. 'My dear Twinks, what a pleasure it is to hear from you. In Oxford, I find I am constantly surrounded by the babbling of second-rate minds. What a blessed relief it is to talk to someone who is my intellectual equal.'

She made no comment on what he said. It had never been her habit to be coy about accepting compliments, particularly when – as in this case – he spoke no less than the truth. 'Razzy,' she said, 'I wonder if I could impose on your good nature to do some research for me?'

'It would be no imposition at all. It has to be more interesting than what I have on my desk right now.'

'Why, what are you working on?'

'Oh, it's just a petition I've had from the League of Nations. They want my advice on how to achieve world peace. Boring, boring, boring.' There was the sound of a considerable tonnage of papers hitting the floor. 'There! All that's off my desk. So, what do you want me to research for you, Twinks?'

'It concerns a lump of toadspawn who's running various wocky operations in London.'

'Excellent! Much more interesting. As you know, I have extensive contacts in the London underworld.'

'That's why I'm asking you, Razzy. I knew it'd be your size of pyjamas.'

'So, what's the name of the rotter you want me to spill the beans on?' There was a new excitement in the voice of Professor Erasmus Holofernes. World peace could go hang. This was the kind of investigation that really got his juices flowing.

Twinks replied, 'Barmy Evans.'

There was a long silence, and when the Professor answered, it was in a much more subdued tone. 'I don't need to do any extra research to tell you about him, Twinks.'

And he spelled out to her the full extent of Barmy Evans's evil.

While there have been many politicians who have used their position to further their criminal intentions, there have been relatively few criminals whose motivation was political. But Barmy Evans was one of that select band.

It did, though, take a while for Blotto to work this out. But then it took a while for Blotto to work most things out.

One of the reasons for his slowness of perception in this particular case was that Blotto's own political convictions were rather vague. In fact, if he were ever asked about the subject, he would probably have said that he didn't have any politics. He had just grown up believing the obvious: that, by birth, the aristocracy were superior to everyone else, so it was natural that they should own more land and money than everyone else, and it was equally natural that everyone else should work very hard to maintain the aristocracy in the manner to which, over the centuries, they had become accustomed. Within his social circle, Blotto very rarely met anyone who thought any differently.

So, the conversation of Barmy Evans was a bit of a revelation to him. Not a revelation in the sense of something that would change his way of thinking (nothing would do that), but a revelation that the world could contain pot-brained pineapples who might actually believe the kind of meringue Barmy spouted out.

'The fact that a toff like you thinks he can take advantage of a girl like Dolly Diller is typical of the corrupt values what we see too much of in this country.'

'I didn't "take advantage" of her,' protested Blotto. 'I just thought she was a bit of a breathsapper, and it'd be creamy éclair to share nosebags with her. I didn't know I was treading on your private bit of lawn. Otherwise I would have taken off my golf shoes.'

'Well, you just be careful. Like I say, Dolly Diller's under my protection, and nobody messes with her. One of the other girls in the revue got uppity with Dolly – girl got sent a bullet to show she was treading on dangerous ground. She backed off; Dolly hasn't had any more trouble from her.'

Blotto knew he was talking about Frou-Frou Gavotte, but didn't have time to make any comment, as Barmy Evans went on, 'You toffs have never thought about other people, never noticed anyone except for your own inbred chinless relatives. Well, that's all going to change! The French got things right.'

'What, you mean by having so many kinds of cheese?'

'No. And the Russkies have got it right, and all.'

'What, by having so many kinds of vodka?'

'No! By having blooming revolutions! String up the aristos! Get them to the guillotine! Line them up against the walls and shout "Fire!".'

'Yes, Mr Evans, I know things like that have happened in France and Russia, but the lumps of toadspawn there are foreign, so what do you expect? That kind of wocky behaviour's never happened in the good old GB.'

'No? You seem to be forgetting we did once shorten one of our Kings by a head.'

'Yes.' Blotto had retained just about enough from what the history beaks had taught him at Eton to say, 'But it didn't catch on. We pretty soon had another King zapping back on to the throne. And that's the track, I'm glad to say, we've been pongling along ever since.'

'Well, it's all about to change.'

Blotto chuckled. 'Sorry, me old thimble, change is one of the things we just don't do in England.'

'You take my word for it. Let me tell you, I have built up the most ruthlessly efficient criminal network London has ever seen.'

It seemed churlish not to offer some kind of compliment, so Blotto said, 'Give that pony a rosette.'

'And so far,' Barmy Evans went on, 'the aim of my enterprise has been just to make money. Well, I've got enough money now. Too much, to be frank.'

'So, what? Are you going to give some of the old jingle-jangle back to the poor pineapples you snaffled it from?'

'No, of course I'm blooming not! I'm going to invest in building a fairer society!'

'Sounds a jolly good wheeze,' said Blotto heartily. 'So long as you make sure the aristocracy are still in charge, you won't put an edge of a toenail wrong.'

'The aristocracy will not still be in charge!' Barmy Evans roared with sudden fury. He crossed to a desk in the corner of the room, rolled down the lid, and locked it. 'In there are my master plans. The aristocracy don't know what's about to hit them. I am already working to weaken their hold on power.'

'How? Oh, I see. You're involved in this devious frolic of Everard Stoop and Pierre Labouze, aren't you? Getting aristocrats to twiddle the old reef-knot with showgirls, and diluting the breeding stock that way. Won't work, I'm afraid. English aristocracy's been self-diluting ever since Will the Conk. Marrying unsuitable females, running strings of mistresses, sprogs the wrong side of the blanket . . . it's all happened many times before. Strengthened the spoffing stock, I'd say, rather than diluting it. You won't roll up the map of the aristocracy that way.'

'Never mind that.' Barmy Evans raised his gun, until it pointed straight at Blotto's chest. 'My more immediate concern is how I'm going to deal with you.'

Detective Inspector Craig Dewar had suggested they meet in a small all-night café near Piccadilly Circus. It only had one entrance, and the minute Twinks walked through the door, she knew she had stepped into a trap.

Because the man who greeted her, and identified himself as the Inspector, only came up to her shoulder. She knew that there was a minimum height requirement of five foot ten inches for English policemen, so the idea that the short man in front of her had any connection to Scotland Yard was laughable.

He had the nerve to introduce himself as 'Detective Inspector Craig Dewar'.

'Puddledash!' said Twinks. 'You're no more a policeman than I am. You just pretended to be a cop, so that my brother would tell you how things were going in our investigation.'

The little man grinned. 'Yes, and that's exactly what he did. Very obliging chap, your brother.' He stepped forward. 'And now I think it's time that you joined him.'

Twinks turned to rush from the café, but outside, waiting for her, were two men in black overcoats, with black hats pulled down over their eyes. Though she carried a variety of weapons in her sequinned reticule, Twinks made no attempt to evade capture. Like Blotto before her, she reckoned being abducted would get her closer to the villains she was after. She made no fuss about getting into a black saloon with tinted windows, along with the two men in black and the false Inspector Dewar.

17

To Catch an Earl

It was a phone call that had got Blotto off the hook. Just as it looked as though Barmy Evans was about to shoot him, the villain had been interrupted by the ringing from the hall. Though Blotto didn't know, the call was from the man he knew as Detective Inspector Craig Dewar, who was announcing that he'd captured Twinks, and asking his boss what to do with her.

Barmy Evans told his subordinate to bring their latest captive to the house where he was holding Blotto and Whiffler. He would deal with all three of them together in the morning.

The result of this was that, sometime during the night, Blotto woke up to find his sister in the same room as him, handcuffed to the middle of the same radiator. He couldn't have been happier.

'It's heaven on a pickle-fork to see you, Twinks me old nail-file,' he enthused.

'Yes, Blotto me old back-scratcher. The fact remains, though, that we are in something of a fumacious treacle-tin.' Her customarily sunny mood had been shadowed by what Professor Erasmus Holofernes had told her about the full extent of Barmy Evans's villainy.

'Oh, come on, tickle up your mustard, sis! Unarmed, chained to a radiator, in the hands of a homicidal lunatic with a gun and a battalion of men in black armed to the teeth – those are the kind of odds we Lyminsters relish!'

'Tickey-Tockey,' said Twinks, though without the vim she usually put into a 'Tickey-Tockey'.

'Well, I'm rolling on camomile lawns,' said Blotto. 'Now we're both here, nobody can defeat us. You and I, Twinks, we could take on the hordes of Genghis Corn.'

'Khan, I think,' suggested Twinks.

'Whoever. You know the boddo I mean.'

'Yes.'

'Well, I'm going to shut the odd eye. So that I'm ready for whatever tomorrow's first bird-burp will bring.'

And Blotto went straight to sleep.

His sister, however, lay awake for quite a long time. Planning how to defeat the greatest evil on earth.

The Reverend Enge operated out of a small church in the City of London, called St Peter-Under-the-Counter. It was there that he conducted the aristocrat-to-showgirl weddings which proved such a lucrative sideline for Everard Stoop and Pierre Labouze. He also officiated at funerals, of the kind at which the mourners did not wish to be publicly seen. Some of these might proceed in the absence of the deceased (in the event, say, that the dearly departed had ended his life in the Thames, attached to a barrel of cement). But they were all done according to the dictates of the Book of Common Prayer.

There were other services, ones not involving prayer books, that the Reverend Enge provided in St Peter-Under-the-Counter. Behind the altar, for example, was one of the best-stocked armouries in London. And the niche in which a statue of St Peter stood, blessing his flock, also contained a large percentage of the illegal drugs available in the metropolitan area. At Communion in St Peter-Under-the-Counter, rather than wafers, many of the faithful were offered small envelopes of white powder.

The Reverend Enge was one of those vicars who believed that his ministry should centre on the community, and, in his case, it was the criminal community.

So it was no surprise that the venue was St Peter-Under-the-Counter, early the following morning, where he briefed his men in black about the forthcoming abduction of the Earl of Hartlepool. There were, incidentally, more men in black than the two who had abducted and guarded Whiffler Tortington. Barmy Evans commanded a nation-wide army of such villains.

Needless to say, the Reverend Enge had inside knowledge about their quarry's movements during the day ahead. Barmy Evans paid informants in all the major London gentlemen's clubs, who provided him with much useful dirt about the doings of the hated aristocracy.

So the aspiring abductors knew that that day the Earl of Hartlepool would be visiting his Jermyn Street pipe-maker to restock with matches for his model of Little Tickling. He would next go to his tailor in Savile Row to be measured for a new morning suit to wear at his forthcoming wedding to Twinks. After that, he had a table booked at Rules for lunch with the Countess of Lytham St Annes. And his chauffeur would then drive him back to Little Tickling in the Rolls-Royce.

Except, of course, the villains in St Peter-Under-the-Counter would see to it that the Earl's schedule was never completed. The men in black took idle bets with each other as to how far through his itinerary the Earl would get before he was abducted. The general view was that he wouldn't make it past Jermyn Street.

The Earl of Hartlepool could not fault the breakfast served that Saturday morning in the Biddles dining room, but he felt restless. His trip to London had been successful. He had got the EGGS committee to set up a subcommittee about the definition of the word 'gun'. He had successfully negotiated with the Dowager Duchess of Tawcester about his marrying her daughter. The only other task he'd set himself before he left Little Tickling was to replenish his stocks of matches in the arcade off Jermyn Street.

So he now rather regretted the appointment he'd made with his tailor and the luncheon engagement at Rules with the Countess of Lytham St Annes. All he wanted to do was to get back to Little Tickling as soon as possible, and start gluing matchsticks on to the vaulted roof of the Winter Ballroom.

Just around the time that the Earl of Hartlepool was settling down to his breakfast at Biddles, in the anonymous prison house, two silent men in black brought Whiffler Tortington back into the room to join Blotto and Twinks. They re-handcuffed him to the unoccupied end of the radiator.

The breakfast on offer there was nothing like the one the Earl was enjoying. On a bench laid parallel to the radiator were placed three bowls of tepid porridge. In their hand-cuffed state, the only way the prisoners could eat was by kneeling and slurping up the food like animals. Twinks was far too sophisticated a creature to descend to such behaviour. Blotto and Whiffler, however, both blessed with hearty appetites, suffered from no such inhibitions. Having wolfed down their own portions, they, with Twinks's permission, took alternate slurps to wolf down hers.

'Now,' she said, when their noisy eating had finished, 'we must focus the brainboxes on how we're going to get out of this swamphole.'

Blotto looked at her expectantly. Long experience had taught him that his sister was only being polite. When she used the plural word 'brainboxes', she didn't include his. Nor in this instance, he reckoned, was she expecting a lot from Whiffler's.

'The first thing to do,' Twinks went on, 'is to get out of these handcuffs.'

'Easier said than done.' Whiffler groaned. 'I've spent the night trying to work my way out of them and got nothing for my pains except more pain. My wrists are shredded. The cuffs're as tight as a nun's drawers.'

'Oh, we can get out of them as easy as raspberries,' said Twinks airily.

'Well, then let's get out of them!' cried Whiffler in desperation.

'No rush,' said Twinks. 'The more important question is: what do we do *once* we've got out of them?'

'We depart this murdy place,' said Blotto, 'find Corky Froggett and the Lag and zap back to Tawcester Towers, like hares on roller skates.'

'And I,' said Whiffler, his anguish giving way to senti-mentality, 'find Frou-Frou Gavotte, and marry her as quick as a lizard's lick.'

'No, we don't do either of those things,' said Twinks. 'First, we have to foil the horracious plot which that lump of toadspawn Barmy Evans is about to inflict on the civilised world.'

'What is his plot?' asked Blotto.

So Twinks told them. She repeated every ghastly detail that Professor Erasmus Holofernes had revealed to her. Both of her listeners were so appalled that they were momentarily deprived of speech.

'You see,' Twinks concluded, 'that's the kind of Grade Z stencher we're up against. We can't think of getting back to Tawcester Towers – or getting married – until we've put some permanent chocks in his cogwheel, can we?'

'No, by Denzil!' said Blotto enthusiastically.

'No,' said Whiffler, with less enthusiasm.

'If only we knew precisely how Barmy Evans was going to start his campaign of evil . . .'

'Yes, that would be a handy handle,' Blotto agreed.

Further discussion was suspended by the entrance into the room of their two guards. One man in black turned to the other and said, 'See, they are talking. Just like the boss said they would be.'

'He said "plotting".'

'Right. And he doesn't want them plotting.'

'Which is why he wants us to sit in here with them.'

It was a long, slow morning. Twinks tried to make conversation with the guards but didn't get any change out of them. And the three prisoners couldn't really discuss their escape plans with the men in black there. Whiffler daydreamed of Frou-Frou Gavotte, and Blotto tried to put the dates of his first-class cricket centuries in order.

Twinks did have a variety of plans to ensure their release – she had long since worked out how to get away from the guards – but she didn't want to implement them yet. She wanted to wait until Barmy Evans was there. Because she was absolutely certain that, sooner or later, he would be.

Like a lot of inordinately wealthy people, the Earl of Hartlepool was constantly in fear of chicanery. He had been known to measure the amount of space in the top of milk bottles to ensure that he wasn't being short-changed. And he brought this same level of paranoid caution to the business of buying matches.

His attitude in such matters was more complex than simple meanness. Had the price of the goods been his main priority, he could have bought his matches considerably cheaper at the average street-corner tobacconist. But though the Earl insisted on paying a Jermyn Street pipe-maker's prices, he remained wary of their cheating him.

The staff of that respectable establishment were well used to his little ways and, given the size of his regular orders, prepared to indulge them. Most of their out-of-town customers would send letters detailing their requirements. A few of the more daringly modern of them would order by telephone. But they knew that the Earl of Hartlepool would always conduct his business in person.

And his regular orders were so large that they had to increase their stock considerably when he announced that he would be paying them a visit.

Once the proprietor of the pipe-maker had discovered the purpose to which the noble Earl was putting his purchases and, since the volume of boxes had to be ordered specially, he had put to the customer the suggestion that the matchsticks could be delivered without flammable tips, thus saving him the trouble of cutting those off before gluing the headless sticks in place on his model.

The reaction this proposal received was as incandescent as the flare of one of their overpriced matches. The proprietor was told in no uncertain – in fact, extremely certain – terms to mind his own spoffing business. For the Earl, cutting the head off each individual match was a part of his creative ritual. Woe betide the person who tried to tell him how to make his own model.

The resulting brouhaha nearly saw the end of the commercial relationship between Jermyn Street and Little Tickling. It took a grovelling letter from the company's Managing Director and a gratis delivery of the next order of matches to stroke the ruffled feathers back into place. And it did nothing to diminish the Earl's suspicions of his supplier.

In anticipation of his arrival at the pipe-maker in the arcade off Jermyn Street, the order of matchboxes had been piled up on one of the counters. Since there were a thousand of them, the height of the stack was considerable.

The proprietor greeted his noble customer fulsomely and stood back to watch the routine which invariably ensued. The Earl would begin by counting the number of boxes. Though he always threatened that he would do this individually, box by box, every time he ended up multiplying the numbers visible on the three sides of the cube.

He was less prepared, however, to take the contents of each box on trust. They bore on the outside the legend: 'Average Contents 48', and he had, after the headless-match-suggestion debacle, proposed to open every box to check he wasn't being diddled. Even now, he never opened fewer than five boxes to estimate the accuracy of this claim. Then, on the back of an envelope, he would work out whether the average actually did come to forty-eight.

Which it always did. The pipe-maker in the arcade off Jermyn Street was too concerned with its reputation to risk giving short measure.

Once the Earl was satisfied that the order met his requirements, he would sign a cheque to settle the bill. Then, after he had left, the pipe-maker's staff would take the matchboxes out of the shop and put them in the dickie of the ancient Rolls-Royce waiting, with its patient chauffeur, at the Jermyn Street end of the arcade.

Preoccupied with his counting and cheque-signing that particular morning, the Earl of Hartlepool did not notice the large gathering of men in black in the arcade outside the pipe-maker's. And, since he was unaware that there was anything he needed to evade, the suggestion he put to the proprietor was not part of any evasion tactic.

'Next port of call's my tailor in Savile Row. Be quicker if I go out the back way.'

The proprietor assented readily. He was always relieved when his most lucrative client left the premises. So he ushered the Earl of Hartlepool out of the back door into a little alleyway that linked up with Piccadilly.

It took a while before a member of the Reverend Enge's army noticed that they could no longer see their quarry inside the shop. At once, all drawing their revolvers, the men in black rushed in.

They made all the staff raise their hands, and demanded forcibly to be told where the Earl of Hartlepool had gone. The proprietor, realising that the invading troops wished no good to his best customer, prevaricated to buy time.

This did not go down well with the most hot-headed of the men in black, who reckoned the sound of a gunshot might speed up the proprietor's processes of recollection. He discharged a couple of warning shots into the pile of matchboxes.

In cricketing circles, there is a much-repeated story of a batsman whose trousers burst into flames because a ball struck him on the pocket in which he was carrying a box of 'non-safety' matches. Whether true or – more probably – apocryphal, it does make the point that matches can be ignited by a sharp concussion rather than the traditional striking against a rough surface.

Now, though a single match-head, when struck, creates only a small flame, adequate for the lighting of a pipe, a candle or a gas ring, the effect of more of them igniting simultaneously is more dramatic. And the effect of a bullet crashing into a thousand boxes of them, each containing an average of forty-eight matches, is nothing less than cataclysmic.

So it proved in what had, only minutes before, been a pipe-maker's shop in an arcade off Jermyn Street.

The Earl heard a dull boom from somewhere. He looked up at the perfect blue sky, in anticipation of the accompanying lightning flash, then remembered that lightning had a habit of coming before thunder. Strange, he thought, as he continued blithely towards his tailor in Savile Row.

18

The Map of Doom

It was hard to estimate who was the most bored – Blotto, Twinks and Whiffler, or the two men in black under instructions to stop them plotting. As the stomach-rumbles around the room became more frequent, it was the guards that cracked first. 'We're going to the kitchen now,' said one.

'To make some more ham sandwiches,' said the other.

Whiffler Tortington groaned. He had suffered more than the new arrivals from the constant diet of ham sandwiches (without mustard, by all that's holy!).

'So, no talking,' the first guard told them.

'Or plotting,' added his colleague, as they both left the room.

Obviously ignoring their strictures, Twinks immediately whispered, 'I've had it going round and round in my mind all morning. Even though we know what Barmy Evans is out to achieve, we don't know what'll be his first move.'

'No, we're right the wrong end of the sink plunger there,' Blotto agreed.

'Up a gum-tree without a paddle,' Whiffler added.

Twinks's perfect forehead wrinkled in frustration. 'If only we knew his master plan . . .'

'Yes, if only we did,' Blotto agreed. 'But we're as much in the dark as a black cat in a coal cellar with a mask on.'

Then, very slowly, like the sun emerging from behind a cloud and irradiating the surface of a lake, recollection smoothed his furrowed brow. 'Actually, Twinks me old egg-poacher, I do know *where* his master plan is.'

There was no point in her berating him for not mentioning this fact earlier. But once he had told her, it was a matter of moments for Twinks to produce from her sequinned reticule a set of skeleton keys. With one, she deftly released herself from the handcuffs. She then quickly found the right one to unlock the roll-top desk in the corner of the room.

She extracted a sheaf of papers, including a large folded map. This she opened, and what she saw provoked a very unladylike 'Great whiffling water rats!'

'What is it?' demanded Blotto. 'Come on, uncage the ferrets!'

'Wait, Blotters. There's a lot of guff here I've got to cram in the brainbox. I'll hit you with the headlines when I've read it all.'

'Twinks,' asked Whiffler, rather plaintively, 'couldn't you just let us out of these bracelets?'

'No,' she said. 'First things first.'

She read in silence for a full five minutes, impervious to the pleading expressions on the faces of her two manacled companions. Then, just when she was about to speak, hearing the exterior door of the house being opened, she quickly replaced the papers, relocked the desk, and attached her handcuffs back to the radiator. She had only just completed these manoeuvres when the room door opened to admit Barmy Evans.

'Good morning,' he said, with a joviality which didn't reach as far as his eyes.

Having been duly measured up for his wedding suit, the Earl then made his way to Rules. He had rather regretted agreeing to the luncheon date with the Countess of Lytham

St Annes, but in the event, it proved to be a pleasant – and illuminating – encounter. He was in a considerably more composed mood as he got into the Rolls-Royce in which his chauffeur had been patiently waiting throughout the lunch.

Since he had enjoyed a couple of pre-prandial Scotches, the lion's share of a bottle of 1889 Mouton Rothschild, and a couple of post-prandial cognacs, the Earl was in no mood for conversation. 'Don't talk to me till we get to Little Tickling,' he said.

The chauffeur, brought up from birth to habits of obedience, did as instructed. So the Earl of Hartlepool remained blissfully unaware that there were no matchboxes in the Rolls-Royce. Or indeed that the pipe-maker's shop where he had purchased them no longer existed.

Barmy Evans, on the other hand, had heard what happened in the arcade off Jermyn Street, and was very unhappy about it. He accused Blotto and Twinks of somehow being involved in causing the conflagration. Both were able, in all honesty, to deny the charge, but Evans clearly didn't believe them.

'Anyway, it doesn't matter,' he snarled. 'Your fate has already been decided, the fate of you and all the rest of the useless spongers. I've just moved my schedule forward a bit, that's all.'

'Your schedule being to take the jam off the biscuit for all the aristocrats in this country?' suggested Twinks coolly.

Evans looked slightly surprised at how much she knew, but came back hard with, 'Exactly that!'

'And I would rather imagine,' Twinks went on, 'it's creamy éclair for you that today's a Saturday.' Again, he looked taken aback. 'With the House of Lords not sitting, and its members having pongled back to their country estates ... where you can clamp the bracelets on all of them.'

166

'How do you know all this?' Barmy Evans could not stop himself from looking across to the locked roll-top desk. With sudden anger, he demanded, 'Has one of the guards been talking?'

'No, no, you can't blame your brain-bereft bouncers for this.' Twinks looked magnificent as she faced up to the villain. 'I've just done a lot of research, and I know everything about your murdy machinations.'

'Oh yes?'

'Yes, in deed and word. I know about your map of all the stately homes on the British Isles.'

Again, he asked, 'How? How do you know that?'

'Let's just say that I've got a power which, compared to yours, is a Howitzer to a pea-shooter.' She, too, looked at the roll-top desk. 'You understand the principle of this new discovery of the X-ray, don't you, Mr Evans?'

'I've heard of it,' he conceded.

'Well, I have X-ray powers in my eyes. And nothing as shimsy as a locked desk can prevent me from reading your secret plans.' Twinks wasn't quite sure why she was following this track of nonsense, but she was enjoying herself.

And it did seem to be having the effect of throwing Barmy Evans off his stroke. But only for a moment. Soon he came back forcibly at her. 'I don't care if you know all about my plans. What's more important is that they're already under way, and you're in no position to do anything about stopping them.'

'I wouldn't be so sure about that,' said Twinks, with a confidence she did not really feel.

'Huh,' Evans said sardonically. 'Since you know all about my plans, I take it you know about the Black Marias.'

'Bong on the nose I do,' said Twinks, still sounding cool. 'You've got men stationed all over the country waiting to liberate the Black Marias from the various local constabularies.'

Barmy Evans grinned. 'The process has already started. This morning the Reverend Enge issued instructions from St Peter-Under-the-Counter. By now all of Scotland Yard's Black Marias are in the hands of my men. And all over the country, the same thing is happening.'

Something in what Evans said struck Whiffler as odd. 'Rein in the roans for a moment there. I thought you said you've just moved the schedule forward . . . ?'

'Yes, I have.'

'Well, how do all your team of stenchers round the country know that? Have you written letters to them about the plan?'

Barmy Evans laughed out loud at this outdated concept. 'Certainly not. I am using the very latest in wireless telegraphy to contact my men. It is a system developed by Scotland Yard and installed in all the country's Black Marias, but which I have stolen from them. Within each group, there is one van full of electrical equipment. This means that they can all receive my latest instructions instantly. They had the order to take over the Black Marias early this morning. And just before I came here this afternoon, I issued the order for the Black Marias to advance on the stately homes of England.'

Blotto had heard enough. 'You four-faced filcher!' he shouted. 'The British aristocracy has survived worse than you can throw at them. We didn't come through the Crusades and the Wars of the Roses and the Civil War to have our fetlocks hobbled by some jumped-up little Welshman!'

'The ruination of you toffs has commenced! It is already under way!'

'What is?'

'The Revolution!'

'You running sore!' said Blotto. 'How dare you use a word like that when there's a lady present?'

'I don't care about ladies! I don't care about lords! Do you know where I grew up?'

'No, and I don't particularly want to.'

'Have you ever been to Wales?'

Blotto grimaced. 'No, by Denzil! Why in the name of raspberries would anyone want to go there?'

'Do you know what coal is?'

'Don't change the subject, Mr Evans.'

'Come on, Mr Lyminster. Do you know what coal is?'

'Well, of course I do. Dirty black stuff that heats up the Tawcester Towers plumbing.'

'But I bet a privileged toff like you doesn't even know where coal comes from,' snarled Evans.

'Of course I do. I'm not a complete voidbrain!'

This assertion was arguable, but the master criminal was not about to take issue with it. Instead, he asked, 'All right, where does it come from then?'

'Oh, for the love of strawberries!' said the exasperated Blotto. 'It comes from the coal cellar!'

'No! It comes from the bowels of the earth, where it's dug out by Welsh coal miners.'

'Does it really?' Blotto was taken aback by this novel concept.

'Yes. But not for much longer. That is all going to stop.'

'No more coal mining?' said Whiffler, who was marginally quicker on the uptake than Blotto. 'But surely, that'll mean no more coal?'

'No, it won't,' said Barmy Evans, with grim satisfaction. 'There'll still be coal, but it'll be dug out of the ground by different people.'

'Who?' asked Blotto.

Evans looked ironically at Twinks. 'You know, don't you? Since your X-ray vision has managed to read all my plans.'

'I know what you're planning,' said Twinks, 'but it will never work.'

'Oh, no?'

'No.'

Blotto was a bit confused. 'Sorry, I'm not on the same

169

page here? What is he planning to do? Swap all the Welsh miners for Scottish miners?'

Barmy Evans let out a harsh laugh and said to Twinks, 'Tell him.'

'The master plan,' she said, 'is to capture all of the country's aristocrats, and put them to work in the coal mines. And then to give all of their stately homes to the coal miners.'

'Rats-in-a-sandwich!' said Whiffler. 'That sounds like . . . Socialism!'

'Wash your mouth out, me old muffin-toaster,' said Blotto reprovingly. 'That's another word that shouldn't really be heard when there are ladies present.'

'Sorry, old man, got carried away. Wasn't thinking.'

'Fully understand,' said Twinks.

'Thanks,' said Whiffler. 'You're a Grade A foundation stone to take it like that.'

'No icing off my birthday cake,' said Twinks.

'Listen!' roared Barmy Evans. 'Will you load of toffs just put a sock in it! What I came to tell you is that one of Scotland Yard's finest Black Marias will be here in a matter of minutes to take you lot off to Wales.'

'Hold back the hounds a moment,' said Blotto, who had been slowly processing what he had recently heard. ''You're saying that Black Marias are on their way to capture the aristocrats in every stately home in the country . . . ?'

'Yes,' Barmy Evans confirmed.

'Including Tawcester Towers?'

The villain grinned and fondled his moustache, as he confirmed this.

'And you're planning to capture the Mater, and Loofah – he's my brother, the Duke – and Sloggo his wife, and all their girls, and take them off to work in Welsh coal mines?'

'That's exactly what I'm planning to do. I'm glad the message has finally sunk in. And then I will take over the government of this country!'

'But . . . but . . .' Blotto did his goldfish impression. 'You can't do that.'

An evil grin played around Barmy Evans's lips as he asked, 'How're you going to stop me?'

'Well,' said Twinks, 'I might have a few ideas.'

19

Secrets of the Sequinned Reticule

Before Barmy had time to react, she had managed to reach into her sequinned reticule and produce a self-igniting firecracker. In the seconds during which he was dazzled by the flash, she again used the skeleton keys to undo her handcuffs.

But, when the smoke cleared, she hadn't had time to do the same service for Blotto and Whiffler. The revolver was once again in Barmy Evans's hand, and a shout had summoned the two men in black from their ham-sandwich-making (without mustard) duties. They too had guns at the ready.

'Shoot them!' shouted their boss. 'They're more trouble than they're worth!'

Another firecracker from the sequinned reticule bought a few more seconds' respite, but Twinks didn't use the time to free her accomplices. Instead, she reached back into the reticule and produced a set of monkey wrenches. She worked quickly behind the radiator with these, then stepped meekly forward and held up her hands, as the three revolver barrels focused on her.

'Shoot me first,' said Twinks.

'Why should we do that?' asked Barmy Evans.

'Oh, for the love of cheese!' she responded. 'Don't they

teach you any manners in Wales? You should know, the rule is always: "Ladies first".'

'OK, boyos,' said Barmy. 'We all shoot together!'

As the three revolvers were levelled at her chest, Twinks suddenly pulled a thin chain lasso from her sequinned reticule. She whirled it up to fix securely to the light fitting, then lifted herself high above the ground, just as the three guns fired in unison. The three bullets clanged against the radiator, in front of which she'd been standing.

'Jollissimo!' cried Twinks from near the ceiling. 'Forward into battle, lads!'

As she started to sing 'The British Grenadiers' –

'Some talk of Alexander, and some of Hercules . . .'

– Blotto and Whiffler surged ahead.

The monkey wrench had loosened the radiator from its fixings, and the handcuffs of the two men lifted it from the ground. Steaming water hissed from a broken pipe, as the heavy metal rectangle swung forward. It connected first with Barmy Evans's shins and, as he fell, clattered into the two men in black. Three revolvers went flying through the air.

The radiator came to a rest on the other side of the room, just as Twinks concluded the chorus of the song: . . .

'There's none that can compare,
With a tow, row row row, row row row,
To the British Grenadiers!'

And she sang it as Honoria Lyminster, not Florrie Coster.

Deftly, she replaced the chain lasso in her sequinned reticule and, extracting the skeleton keys, released her two companions from their handcuffs. It was a matter of moments to transfer the three sets of bracelets to the three dazed villains and handcuff them to the now-freestanding radiator. Taking a larger chain from her reticule, Twinks fixed it round the radiator, which she padlocked to a solid water pipe.

Picking up the three revolvers, she dropped them neatly into her sequinned reticule. She extracted her set of skeleton keys, and opened the roll-top desk to appropriate Barmy Evans's map and plans.

'Right, gentlemen,' she said. 'Time we left this fumacious swamphole and rescued our country from the ravages of Socialism!'

'Toad-in-the-hole!' said her brother, lost in admiration. 'You really are quite a girl.'

'Don't talk such toffee,' said Twinks, as she led them out of the room.

The three men attached to the radiator were still too dazed to offer anything by way of riposte.

20

Saviours of the Aristocracy

When the escapees emerged, Twinks recognised that the street they were on was near the Church Institute in Fulham, where she had recently expended so much effort rehearsing. But it wasn't the moment to philosophise about how close she had been all that time to the imprisoned Whiffler. There were more urgent priorities.

'We need to get to Little Tickling zappity-ping,' Twinks announced. 'According to his plans, that's Barmy Evans's first priority. Once his blunderthugs have captured the Earl of Hartlepool, the order will go out to attack all the other stately homes.'

'Pardon my poke-in, Twinks me old collar stud,' said Blotto. 'Shouldn't we be shifting our shimmies for Tawcester Towers first?'

'No, Blotters. This is a case of FHB.'

'"Family Hold Back"? But why?'

'Because the Earl at Little Tickling is less well protected. Oliver Cromwell emptied the place in short order during the Civil War, whereas he couldn't shift a single Lyminster from Tawcester Towers. Anyway, you forget who they'll encounter when they reach the old homestead. Can you really see Barmy Evans's mercenaries making the Mater budge an inch?'

'Good ticket, Twinks. Little Tickling it is. How're we

going to get there? The Lag's at the Savvers. Can we get a cab there?'

'Not round here, we can't,' said Whiffler. 'No self-respecting taxi driver would venture out somewhere as squalid and dangerous as Fulham.'

'No,' Blotto agreed, with a sigh. 'So, we're as stumped as a pirate with two wooden legs.'

'Puddledash!' said Twinks. 'When we Lyminsters see a problem, we don't skirt round it – we dig our heels into our charger's flanks, and we gallop straight through!' She pointed to a black saloon parked directly outside the house. It had tinted windows and the engine was running. 'What was that thing Dolly Diller said to you, Blotters . . . about having a "special taxi service"?'

Twinks stepped forward and tapped on the driver's window. Though he was initially unwilling to take the fare, having three revolver barrels pointed at the back of his neck brought him round to his passengers' point of view.

He agreed to drive them to the Savoy.

Once there, Blotto tried to locate Corky Froggett, but the hotel staff said they had not seen him, and nor had they received any message as to his whereabouts. The Lagonda was, however, still in the Savoy car park.

Blotto looked to his sister for advice.

'Don't don your worry-boots about Corky,' she said crisply. 'You and Whiffler get in the Lag, and drive to Little Tickling like there's a forest fire behind you! Save the Aged P from whatever murdy gluepot Barmy's army are trying to jam him into!'

'Aren't you coming with us, Twinks me old carpet underlay?'

'No, I'll join you there. I've got another little problemette to resolve.'

Blotto did as he was told (which he almost always did when it was his sister issuing the instructions). Grabbing

Whiffler by the arm, he rushed down to the garage. Within minutes, the Lagonda was wolfing down the miles on its way to Little Tickling.

Twinks got a cab to Madame Clothilde of Mayfair. As on her previous visit, the proprietress was not in the salon and had to be summoned from upstairs by one of her elegant acolytes. Again, when she arrived, she displayed a small part of a percentage point less than her customary perfection.

And, once more, she was followed downstairs by a very sheepish-looking Corky Froggett, buttoning up his uniform.

'Twinks,' said Clothilde, 'what is the matter? You look *inquiète*.'

It was true. There was an unaccustomed sheen of perspiration on the fine patrician brow. A very fetching sheen, it goes without saying.

'The fact is, we're neck-deep in a quagmire! The forces of evil are striking at the roots of every family tree in the country!'

'*Sacrebleu!*' said Clothilde.

'Where is the young master?' asked Corky Froggett. 'I need to be at his side in the Lagonda!'

'Afraid you missed the starting pistol on that one. Blotto's already on his way, zappity-ping, to Little Tickling.'

'You mean I have let him down?' asked the chauffeur, pulling his service revolver from a jacket pocket. 'I cannot live with the shame!' And he raised the barrel of the gun to his temple.

'Corkee . . . *non!*' shrieked Clothilde.

'Don't be such a pot-brained pineapple,' said Twinks, firmly removing the revolver from his hand. 'You'll be far more use alive than you will coffinated.'

'Anything I can do, milady . . . for you and the young

master. And if it happens to involve laying down my life for—'

'Stick a toffee up your trombone, Corky! You need to find a car and drive like a galvanised torpedo!'

'To Little Tickling, milady?'

'No, to Tawcester Towers! The stenchers are planning an attack there too!'

'I'm on my way!' said Corky Froggett, racing for the door.

'I will see you soon, *chéri* . . . ?' asked Madame Clothilde.

But the chauffeur made no reply. He was not aware, as he left Madame Clothilde of Mayfair, how many plots of novels, plays and operas concern the conflict between love and duty, but that did not prevent him from feeling somewhat lower than an earthworm for the situation into which he had got himself.

Twinks turned to the couturier and, before the woman had had time to react to her lover's abrupt departure, said, 'And now, Clothilde, there is a very special service I require from you.'

It was more than an hour later that Twinks re-emerged from Madame Clothilde of Mayfair. She took a cab to Warren Street near Euston Square, which was the centre for London's used-car dealers. She told the least shifty salesman she encountered there that she needed the fastest sports car he had. He instantly offered her an Alvis 12/50 TG beetleback, which she accepted with alacrity. And when she offered money, he refused to take it.

Twinks did not put up the hood, and the wind screamed around her head as she challenged the Lagonda for the fastest recorded time from London to Little Tickling.

What she did not know – could not know – was that a black saloon with tinted windows set off from London shortly after her.

21

Confrontation at Little Tickling

For the Earl of Hartlepool, being back in his workshop at Little Tickling engendered a kind of ecstasy. He'd achieved most of what he needed to in the previous few days. His constitutional duty had been performed on the EGGS committee, and having sorted out his wedding plans gave him a great sense of satisfaction. True, he hadn't returned with his new supply of matchsticks, but he still had enough in reserve to keep going for a few weeks (he always over-catered). Above all, he was no longer in London. He was back where he belonged.

He had lit the brazier to melt his pot of hoof glue, and started with his scalpel, removing the heads of matchsticks. When a small pile had accumulated, he swept them with his hand to join the thousands of others in the crate beside his table.

As he worked, the Earl felt the stresses of London slip away from the tense muscles of his bony shoulders. He was where he should be, doing what he should be doing. Soon he would have his tweezers in hand, adding another component to the vaulted roof of his model Winter Ballroom.

So serene was his mood that he was not a little irritated to hear the discreet cough of the butler at his shoulder.

'What is it, Pentecost,' the Earl demanded testily. 'Can't you see I'm busy?'

'I thought it would be appropriate, milord, to mention to you that Little Tickling is under attack.'

'What do you mean – "under attack"? From whom?'

'I had a telephonic communication, milord, from the porter's lodge at the main entrance, to announce that six armoured police vehicles – commonly known, I believe, as Black Marias – have entered the drive.'

'Well, if they're the police, where's the problem? It's probably the usual thing – one of the under-gardeners being drunk and disorderly in the local pub.'

'No, milord. I have reason to believe that the Black Marias have been stolen from the constabulary by criminals, and they are coming to Little Tickling with malicious intent. Fortunately, milord, because the drive is two miles long, I have had time to arrange for the staff to seal off the original castle unit of the building and raise the drawbridge. I need hardly remind you, milord, that during the Wars of the Roses, Little Tickling survived a siege of two hundred and seventeen days.'

'Yes, Pentecost, but we didn't come up to the mark during the Civil War. And, if my recollection of family history is correct, the army besieging Little Tickling during the Wars of the Roses used ladders to try to ascend the castle walls, and were only repulsed by having boiling oil poured over them.'

'That is true, milord.'

'Well, do we have any boiling oil? Or, come to that, cold oil that we could boil?'

'No, milord. But we do have a more modern means of repelling invaders, which was not available during the fifteenth century.'

'What are you talking about, Pentecost?'

'I am talking about guns, milord. I have sent staff to the cellar to collect all of the shotguns that have been in storage there since Your Lordship last gave a shooting party, and distributed them among all the staff, even down to the newest housemaid.'

'I can't allow guns to be used,' said the Earl. 'I'm on the committee of EGGS.'

'But I would have thought, milord, *in extremis*, as we are now—'

'No guns.'

'But if we do not use guns, the criminals will soon gain access.'

'No guns!' the Earl confirmed in a thunderous voice. 'And let down the drawbridge. Let us find out what it is they want. It's probably something completely innocuous.'

It should be said that, in some areas of life, the Earl of Hartlepool was as trusting as a child.

'I was just thinking,' said Blotto, as the Lagonda roared on its way, 'that the last time I pongled along this way, it was to turn out for your team on the Little Tickling cricket pitch. Tickle the old memory buds?'

'Vaguely,' said Whiffler.

'Which reminds me, actually, me old muffin-toaster, I haven't yet had an invitation to play for you this year.'

'No,' Whiffler agreed. 'The fact is, Blotto . . .'

'Yes?'

'Since I've met Frou-Frou, I've rather lost interest in cricket.'

'Toad-in-the-hole!' Blotto knew his friend was in a bad way, but he hadn't begun to realise it was *that* bad.

The Earl of Hartlepool and his butler stood at the castle end of the lowered drawbridge, as the fleet of six Black Marias came to a halt on the Little Tickling drive. Behind them, inside the castle, stood many very frustrated Little Tickling staff. History, among other things, told them that they could easily see off this invasion, but the Earl had ordered them to lay down their arms. And at Little Tickling, everyone did what the Earl said.

The leading Black Maria looked different from the other five, chiefly because a large network of aerials was poking out of its roof. It was from this vehicle that a small figure stepped out and walked slowly towards the entrance.

'Good afternoon,' he said. 'I'm Detective Inspector Craig Dewar of Scotland Yard.'

The Earl looked triumphantly at his butler. 'See, Pentecost, I told you they'd be legitimate police officers.'

Twinks had to stop the Alvis 12/50 at an out-of-town garage for petrol. The man who handled the pump and filled her up did not ask her for any payment.

In the gateway of Little Tickling, the Earl, Pentecost and Detective Inspector Craig Dewar all heard the sound of more approaching vehicles. The Inspector knew what was coming, but the other two looked with puzzlement down the long drive.

There were six in this convoy, as there had been with the Black Marias, but they were much more battered and dirty and covered in coal dust. In the open backs of the lorries stood dozens of men, equally battered and dirty and covered in coal dust. Waving picks and shovels in the air, they shouted incomprehensible slogans in Welsh.

'Ah. Good,' said Detective Inspector Craig Dewar. 'Your new tenants have arrived.'

A fusillade of gravel erupted, as the Lagonda turned sharply in through the main gates of Little Tickling. 'Does it set a cockle of your heart simmering to see the old place?' asked Blotto.

'No,' said Whiffler. 'It means nothing to me. I'm still going to renounce the title and marry Frou-Frou!'

Blotto recognised that further conversation on this matter might be required at some point. He also recognised that this wasn't the moment.

Showing the Welsh miners round the interior was not the kind of job that Pentecost favoured, but the men in black all carried revolvers, so he didn't have much choice in the matter. He winced at the footprints of coal dust on the original Axminster carpets of the main reception rooms, and the mucky fingerprints left on the armorial displays. He couldn't understand the comments made in Welsh about the house, but he doubted that they were respectful.

Eventually, all of the men in black and the miners ended up in the former ballroom, which was now the Earl of Hartlepool's workshop. Detective Inspector Craig Dewar looked contemptuously at the matchstick model.

'I had heard rumours that you were building this,' he said, 'but only now do I see that they are actually true. What further proof do we need' – he addressed the assembled throng of miners – 'of the truth of Barmy Evans's arguments. All of you work hard in the pit for a pittance . . . while the aristocracy have nothing better to do than build matchstick models of their own houses! Is that justice?'

The miners must have been bilingual, because they all shouted, 'No!'

'But, fortunately, things are about to change. Justice will be done! You will live here in luxury – ' the miners cheered – 'while the bloated gluttons of inherited wealth . . .'

The Earl looked puzzled rather than upset. He had no idea that the Inspector was referring to him.

'. . . will get their just deserts. By this time tomorrow, the Earl of Hartlepool – and all of those like him – will have started working down the mines!'

'I wouldn't be so sure about that.'

They all looked towards the sound of the voice. With Whiffler Tortington by his side, Blotto had entered the room. And, triumphantly, he was wielding his cricket bat.

Twinks was relieved to see the Lagonda parked in front of Little Tickling and slid the Alvis 12/50 into place beside it. She was less pleased to see the six Black Marias and the six coal lorries, though she had predicted that they would be there.

The positive that she noticed, though, was that all of the enemy vehicles were empty. Whatever was happening was happening inside the building.

Knowing exactly what she was doing, Twinks walked towards the Black Maria that was festooned with aerials, and got into the driver's seat.

Meanwhile, in the Earl of Hartlepool's workshop, Blotto faced about thirty Welsh miners armed with picks and shovels, and about thirty men in black, armed with revolvers. Once again, he was up against the kinds of odds he relished. And this time he had his cricket bat with him.

'Come on, you lumps of toadspawn!' he cried. 'In spite of all the fumacious things you've been saying, I'll show that the British aristocracy still have their uses!'

Two of the men in black crept towards him, revolver barrels homing in on his heart. With one slightly un-orthodox sweep to leg, Blotto's cricket bat sent the guns flying in the air, as the two assailants clutched at their broken wrists.

'Shall we just shoot him, sir?' another man in black asked the false Inspector Dewar.

'No,' came the reply. 'We want him alive. Barmy Evans has a special, personal revenge lined up for those two.'

The small man moved much more quickly than anyone expected him to and was suddenly holding his revolver at the Earl of Hartlepool's temple. 'On the other hand, Barmy doesn't care what happens to this one.' He looked directly at Blotto. 'Put that cricket bat down, or there'll be an empty seat in the House of Lords!'

Blotto looked at his old muffin-toaster for guidance. Though perhaps not as close to his father as some sons, Whiffler still didn't want to see the old man put down like a superannuated carthorse. Reading this in his friend's expression, Blotto dropped his cricket bat. It was immediately picked up by a man in black.

The Little Tickling staff looked pleadingly at the butler and then down at their abandoned shotguns, desperate for his permission to let them defend their heritage. But after a quick glance at the Earl, Pentecost shook his head.

'Right,' said Detective Inspector Craig Dewar, 'let's get the prisoners out of the house. We've got to pick up a few more useless toffs at a few more stately homes on our way to Wales.' He turned to the miners. 'So soon, boys, you'll have free run of this place! And I happen to have heard that this place has one of the best wine cellars in the country.'

Again, though they were largely beer drinkers, the miners cheered, waving picks and shovels in the air, and uttering more incomprehensible bits of Welsh. The men in black closed in on Blotto and Whiffler, two to each, immobilising their arms.

'But, first,' said the Inspector, with sudden malevolence, 'let's get rid of this self-indulgence!' And, lifting a hammer from the workshop table, he brought it down with great force on the model of Little Tickling. Matchsticks flew in every direction.

The effect on the Earl of Hartlepool was instantaneous. He would probably have done the same, had the Inspector's gun still been at his forehead, but of course it no longer was. In a fit of white-hot fury, the Earl snatched down one of the ancient shotguns from its wall bracket and shouted out, 'Staff, pick up your guns! I've had it up to

185

here with EGGS! The kind of man who'd destroy my model deserves no quarter! Let's rid Little Tickling of these oikish sponge-worms!'

He let rip with his shotgun. The pellets flew high over the heads of the crowd, but were a signal for every other gun in the place to be fired. In the ensuing noise and chaos, Blotto and Whiffler managed to break free from their captors. Blotto picked up his cricket bat and burst into the fray, flooring men in black with a variety of hooks and drives.

From her Black Maria, Twinks heard the gunfire begin. Quickly finishing what she had to do, she rushed from the vehicle into the castle.

Inside, it was clear to Blotto that the home side was losing. Though most of the bullets and pellets discharged were air-shots, resulting in flesh wounds, the difference in training between the two sets of combatants was beginning to show. The staff of Little Tickling, though loyal and willing enough, had rarely shot at anything more threatening than a lethargic pheasant. Whereas, Barmy Evans's men in black had spent nearly every night of their lives in gunfights with the most vicious criminals in the country.

Quite swiftly, the local team was disarmed and dragooned against one wall by the invading army. Eventually, only Blotto continued the fight, defending his corner against wave after wave of men in black, all very frustrated by the fact that they had been forbidden to use their guns against him.

'Nice work, *boyos*! I see you're getting on top.'

Distracted by the new, but horribly familiar, voice in the room, Blotto looked up. And in that moment, two men in black wrested the cricket bat from his grasp.

On the other side of the room, his moustache rampant and a smile of triumph spreading across his pockmarked features, stood Barmy Evans.

Broken biscuits, thought Blotto, once again clasped in the vice-like grip of two men in black. And deprived of his cricket bat. I really am in a bit of a swamphole, and no mistake.

He wondered where Twinks was. In the past, Twinks had always managed to get them out of the quaggiest of quagmires. But there was no sign of her.

'Right, *boyos*,' said Barmy Evans, still glowing with his success. 'You've done very well, and soon the order will go out to your colleagues to pick up all the other aristocratic space-wasters in the country. Just a few things that need to be done before that . . . First, a job for you miners. Take all the Little Tickling staff and lock them in the cellar. And make sure none of their weapons go down there with them!'

The miners seemed happy with the job they'd been delegated to do, and the Little Tickling staff were so demoralised by their recent defeat that they submitted meekly to imprisonment.

'Now, men,' said Barmy Evans, once all the miners were out of the room, 'just a slight change of plan. A couple of the coal lorries coming from Wales to get the toffs out of other stately homes have broken down. That means we're going to need this lot of miners as extra muscle. They may not be keen about the delay in taking over this place, but I think I can rely on you lot to persuade them to do as I want.'

There were a few chuckles at this. 'Persuading' was one of their duties that the men in black enjoyed most.

'So, when they come back, I want you to take the miners and put them in the Black Marias. Most of you'll be in there with them, to deal with any trouble.'

Further chuckles. 'Dealing with any trouble' was another part of the job they enjoyed.

'Just so's none of them escape, the designated driver of each vehicle will lock the Black Maria from the outside and unlock it when you reach your destination . . . which I will give you shortly. All got that?'

The men in black mumbled assent. Still feeling slightly cheated by not being allowed to shoot Blotto and Whiffler, they relished the prospect of a little casual violence towards the miners in the Black Marias.

Barmy Evans listened to sounds from the hall. 'Right, the miners are coming back. Could the designated drivers of the Black Marias take over the guarding of the prisoners?'

As the men in black changed roles, one of them asked, 'Where are we going to take the toffs? Which of the Black Marias do you want them in?'

'Not in any of them. You forget, they have a different destination. They're about to find out the delights of coal mining in Wales. When you get outside, you'll find a blue Lagonda parked. Put them in that. And I'll join you there, when we've got the miners locked up.'

Blotto considered making a bid for freedom straight away, but, his mind working well, as it usually did in stressful situations, decided against it. There were too many armed men around. Once they were in the Lagonda, with just Barmy Evans and however many guards he chose to escort them, that would be the time for action.

So he submitted meekly, as did Whiffler and the Earl, to being frogmarched out of Little Tickling.

The three of them seemed to be sitting in the Lagonda for a long time, while Barmy Evans checked that his instructions had been followed in the Black Marias. Outside the car, the six designated drivers stood on guard.

Eventually, they saw Barmy Evans approaching the Lagonda. 'Right, they're all locked in,' he said to the drivers.

'You lot will all find your destinations in envelopes by your steering wheels. Drive straight there. Don't stop for anything.'

The drivers expressed their assent and set off towards their vehicles.

Barmy Evans didn't get into the Lagonda. He just stood there, watching the Black Marias proceeding down the long drive away from Little Tickling. Then he turned and looked at the Lagonda's occupants.

'Don't you think, Mr Evans,' asked Blotto, a supercilious smile tugging at the corners of his mouth, 'that you're taking rather a risk, travelling on your own with us, without any extra guard?'

'Oh, I don't think it's that much of a risk,' said the voice of Twinks, as she stripped Barmy Evans's moustache from her perfect upper lip.

22

All Relatively Tickey-Tockey

As she removed the disgusting make-up of pockmarks and other of Barmy Evans's accoutrements, Twinks observed, 'She is good, Madame Clothilde ... you know, when it comes to disguises.'

'You had the voice and everything,' said Whiffler, lost in admiration.

'Voices are as easy as a housemaid's virtue,' said Twinks.

'Well, I swallowed it, like a trout does a Wickham's Fancy.'

'Yes, having observed the stencher at close quarters,' Blotto agreed, 'I can confirm that you were as alike as two butter pats.'

'As I mentioned,' said Twinks, 'it should be Madame Clothilde you're pinning the rosettes on. Though I must say, pongling round the country dressed as Barmy Evans did just make me realise how far the thimble-rigger's influence extends.'

'Sorry? Not on the same page,' said Whiffler.

Twinks explained about not being charged in Warren Street for the Alvis 12/50 or in the filling station for the fuel. 'Both of them thought I was the real biscuit, and they didn't want to get on the wrong side of Barmy Evans.'

'So, do you reckon the real version of the stencher is still chained to a radiator in Fulham?'

'We can only hope so, Whiffler. We'll get the full SP when we're back in London. So, Blotters, let's get there – zappity-ping!'

'But rein in the roans for a moment there,' said Blotto. 'One thingette I want to de-cobweb ... You just told the Black Maria drivers you'd given them places to go to ...'

'Yes,' Twinks agreed. 'And I have also, using the wireless telegraphy system in the specially adapted Black Maria, given instructions as to where all the others involved in this fumacious plot should go to.'

Blotto looked puzzled. Again. 'And did those instructions come from the real Barmy, or from you?'

'From me. Though, obviously I was using his voice, so all his villains think they came from him.'

'So where have you sent the stenchers?' asked Blotto eagerly.

Twinks smiled a quiet smile. 'Oh, I think we'll find out quite soon enough.'

'Just a minute,' said the Earl of Hartlepool from the back of the car, where he was sitting next to Whiffler. 'Have all those lumps of toadspawn gone?'

'Yes,' said Twinks.

'And they won't be pongling back here in short order?'

'No, they won't.'

'And my staff are still all locked in the cellar, are they?'

'Yes, I'll let the poor greengages out before we go,' said Twinks.

'Don't bother about that,' said the Earl, as he gathered himself up to leave the car. 'I'll do it.'

'Tickey-Tockey.'

'Just a minute,' he said, suddenly intrigued by the face beside him. 'Who're you?'

'I'm your son, Giles.'

'Good heavens! Is that what you look like?'

With that, the Earl of Hartlepool scuttled back inside Little Tickling, to assess the damage and start rebuilding his matchstick model.

And Blotto floored the accelerator of the Lagonda, all the way back to the Savoy.

A few hours before these events, a very subdued Corky Froggett arrived in his hire car at Tawcester Towers. In front of the great house was an array of vehicles similar to those which had parked at Little Tickling. A row of Black Marias, behind which was drawn up a row of coal trucks. Although Corky was not to know it, the same scene was being played out at stately homes all over the United Kingdom.

The vehicles were all empty, except for one. In the front of a Black Maria with a paraphernalia of aerials and wires sprouting out of it, sat a man in black. He was so busy talking into some telephonic device that he did not notice as Corky Froggett walked past him towards the house.

The chauffeur drew his service revolver out of his pocket. The young mistress had instructed him to rescue the Lyminster family, and that was what he would do. Or die in the attempt. As he entered the Great Hall and saw the number of men in black and miners assembled there, the odds on dying in the attempt looked pretty high. Which gave Corky Froggett great satisfaction. He was being offered an opportunity to expiate the sin of not being on hand when the young master needed him.

But he was stopped in his tracks by a voice booming from the other end of the Great Hall. The voice seemed to have stopped everyone else in their tracks too.

It was a voice Corky recognised. At the foot of the great staircase, only requiring a Union Jack shield, a helmet and a trident to complete her Britannia pose, stood the Dowager Duchess. Behind her on the stairs cowered Loofah, the current Duke of Tawcester, his wife Sloggo, and a sprinkling of their daughters.

'And I suggest,' the Dowager Duchess was bellowing, 'that you all turn round and return to the squalid swampholes from which you emerged! Tawcester Towers has lasted too long to be taken over by a common riffraff like you. It has survived being besieged during the Wars of the Roses and again during the Cromwellian unpleasantness. The Lyminster family are also survivors, whose superior breeding has always set them above scum like you. We survive – and will continue to survive – on one simple principle: Keep the serfs down where they belong!'

Corky Froggett, enjoying the good sense that the Dowager Duchess was talking, looked around at the tide of men she was holding back by sheer force of personality. They were all appropriately shamefaced and subdued, rather as the young master and mistress looked when they emerged from a dressing-down by their mother in the Blue Morning Room. On the other hand, most of the men in black carried revolvers, and Corky wondered for how long they would continue to know their place.

Fortunately, before their patience could be put to the test, the chauffeur heard a cry from behind him. The man in black who had been fiddling with the telephony in the Black Maria outside, rushed into the Great Hall, calling out, 'Change of plan!'

The other men in black and the miners turned towards him, as he continued, 'Just had a message from the boss by wireless telegraphy. We're to clear out of this place straight away. There's a new destination he wants us to go to!'

It seemed a matter of seconds until the only occupants of the Great Hall were members of the Lyminster family. And, of course, one of their chauffeurs. Corky, who knew it wasn't his place to be there under such circumstances, silently withdrew.

But, as he left, he heard the Dowager Duchess observing to her son, the Duke, 'It's like dealing with Labrador puppies. Make it clear from the start who's boss, and they won't give you any trouble.'

* * *

At Scotland Yard, and in various county constabularies, there was great consternation. They had hardly recovered from the shock of having every Black Maria in the country stolen, before they had to cope with the surprise of having each last one of them returned.

The drivers from Little Tickling had followed the directions placed in envelopes by their steering wheels, and those outside other stately homes did as they had been told by Barmy Evans's telephonic instructions, broadcast from the Little Tickling Black Maria.

The confusion of the nation's police force quickly turned to jubilation, when they discovered that, locked in the back of the returning Black Marias, were virtually every member of Barmy Evans's gang. They were particularly pleased to have delivered to them a criminal who had had the nerve to pass himself off as one of their own, under the name of Detective Inspector Dewar. It was a network they had been trying, without success, to crack for years.

The jubilation turned to ecstasy when an anonymous tip-off to Scotland Yard told them that the gang's ringleader, Barmy Evans himself, could be found attached to a radiator in a house in Fulham.

Twinks had made the police's job easy for them. All they had to do off their own bat was to organise transport back to Wales of a large number of disgruntled and incomprehensible miners. They all went back down the pits to earn a pittance, and make huge profits for the aristocrats, whose homes they had been so near to taking over. The proper social order had been restored.

So, when the Commissioner for the Metropolitan Police was given a knighthood by a grateful King, 'for his incomparable achievement in rounding up the Barmy Evans gang', it never occurred to the officer in question that anyone else deserved a share of the nation's gratitude.

And when Blotto suggested to his sister that she perhaps

ought to have got some credit for her contribution, all she said was, 'Don't talk such toffee.'

Since before the abduction which had set these adventures in train, Whiffler Tortington's only wish had been to marry Frou-Frou Gavotte, and now there was nothing to stop him from achieving that ambition.

Because, at one point, Barmy Evans had also wanted to effect that union – and had even made some arrangements towards that end – Whiffler contacted the Revd Enge about the wedding arrangements. The clergyman, knowing by then that all of his previous associates – Barmy Evans and the men in black – would soon be in prison, agreed to conduct the ceremony at St Peter-Under-the-Counter. (He also, deprived of other outlets for his talents, had a kind of damascene conversion and embraced the novel idea of devoting the rest of his life to the spiritual welfare of his parishioners.)

The wedding, arranged with all the speed that Whiffler and Frou-Frou could have wished, was a quiet affair. Blotto and Twinks, of course, were present. So were Dippy Le Froom and his new wife Poppy. The *Light and Frothy* company were represented only by Jack Carmichael. Pierre Labouze and Everard Stoop, regarding the marriage as just another transaction in their aristocrat/showgirl business, did not attend. Nor did they find out till afterwards that neither Whiffler nor Frou-Frou had any intention of signing a contract to pass over a percentage of their income to the two schemers.

Logic dictated that they hold the Reception at the Savoy. It was a splendid occasion, at which the champagne flowed generously. There were only two speeches. Jack Carmichael, who had given Frou-Frou away, spoke at some length about what a talented performer he was, but nobody listened. They just went on quaffing champagne.

Everyone was silent, though, when Giles 'Whiffler'

Tortington stood up to speak. Oratory was not really his thing, but the four words he did speak were greeted with massive applause. 'I'm just so happy,' he said, looking at the love of his life.

Blotto had been encouraged, during the Reception, to see Dippy Le Froom knocking back the champagne with the best of them and, after the speeches, got the opportunity for a word alone with his old muffin-toaster.

Nodding towards Poppy, he said, 'I thought that little breathsapper of yours reckoned you didn't need the old alkiboodles.'

Dippy beamed. 'Oh no, she's come round to the idea.'

'How did you swiggle that?'

'Didn't have to. She's just such a sweet, caring girl. All she's concerned about is my happiness. She saw how unhappy I was off the alkiboodles and, as she said, realised that my heart was big enough to love both her and a bottle of good claret. So, she let me off the leash!'

'What a Grade A foundation stone you married there, Dippy.'

'Couldn't agree more. And what's more – another spoffing good bit of news – there's soon going to be a little Le Froom crawling round the carpets.'

'Toad-in-the-hole, Dippy! You *are* the boy!'

'Thanks, Blotters.'

'So, see a lot more of you down the Gren, will we?'

'A bit more.' He looked cautious. 'Fact is, I'll probably be spending more evenings eating at home.'

'Well, I'll be snickered,' said Blotto. 'Are you telling me Poppy's learnt to cook?'

'No, Blotters. Better than that. Again, she suspected something else was making me unhappy, realised – like the little darling she is – what it was putting lumps in my custard. And she asked our chef Xavier to come back!'

Blotto smiled benevolently. There was a God.

Then he remembered that he was shortly going to have to marry Araminta fffrench-Wyndeau and decided that perhaps there wasn't.

The Dowager Duchess did not like going to London, but she suffered from incurable nosiness and, when the Countess of Lytham St Annes invited her to a return luncheon at the Savoy, could not resist agreeing.

Catching sight of her as she processed through the American Bar, Everard Stoop left his cackling acolytes and stepped forward to her. 'Your Grace,' he said, with an inclination of the head, 'a friend in need is a friend whenever you want one.'

'Oh, stuff a pillow in it, you stupid little man!' said the Dowager Duchess, not breaking stride on the way to her table.

There was a look in the eye of the Countess of Lytham St Annes that she didn't like. A look of triumph, as though the Countess had some advantage over her luncheon guest.

'Well, Agatha,' said the Dowager Duchess, 'I trust your little shrimp of a daughter is prepared for her wedding.'

'I can assure you, Evadne, she is fully prepared. And very much looking forward to it.'

'Yes, I did have a thought about her wedding dress.'

'Oh. I would have thought that was a matter in which only *my* thoughts were of importance.'

'Normally, yes, Agatha. But when we're dealing with a child of such an anaemic complexion as your daughter, I think it is only charitable for me to offer you advice.'

'You always think of others, Evadne,' said the Countess through clenched teeth. 'So what advice is it that you have for me?'

'There is a couturier in Mayfair whom my daughter patronises. Her name is Madame Clothilde, and she is a great expert with colour. I think she might have some suggestions to save your daughter on her wedding day from looking like a white sheet of paper wrapped in another white sheet of paper.'

The Dowager Duchess smiled magnanimously as she concluded this advice, but she was slightly disappointed in the Countess's reaction. She had been hoping for blind fury but was rewarded only with slight annoyance. It suggested to the Dowager Duchess the unappealing possibility that her opponent had something up her sleeve.

'Did you . . .' the Countess asked ingenuously, 'like the way the wedding announcement appeared in *The Times*?'

'I did not read it,' came the magisterial response. 'To search for one's own name in the newspapers is a sign of middle-class mediocrity.'

'Yes, I thought you probably hadn't seen it.'

'Oh?'

'In fact, I would have been surprised if you *had* seen it.'

'What are you talking about? Stop shuffling round the shrubbery, Agatha.'

The Countess spoke with agonising slowness. 'I am not surprised that you didn't see the announcement of Araminta and Devereux's engagement in *The Times* . . . because there was no such announcement.'

'What do you mean?'

'I've had a better arfer.'

'I think the word you are looking for is "offer".' She let the idea sink in. 'A better offer?' The Dowager Duchess bubbled like an overheated coffee percolator. 'What do you mean – a better offer?'

'I was always slightly worried about the prospect of Araminta marrying beneath herself.'

'Beneath herself! She would be joining the Lyminster family!'

'Yes, but Devereux is only a younger son. And a younger son of a Dook—'

'The word, Agatha, is "Duke"!'

198

The Countess carried serenely on, 'The younger son of a Dook doesn't cut much mustard these days . . . not for a girl like Araminta. It certainly doesn't compare with her becoming a Countess in her own right.'

'Huh! Your daughter "a Countess in her own right"? And where are you going to find some accommodating Earl ready to take on the anaemic little chit?'

'Oh, don't worry, Evadne. I've found him.'

'What!' The volume of this response attracted looks from all around the Grill Room.

'We sorted out the details,' the Countess of Lytham St Annes went on, 'over lunch at Rules. My daughter Araminta is going to marry the Earl of Hartlepool!'

In her salon in Mayfair, Madame Clothilde opened the envelope the postman had just delivered. She had not recognised the handwriting. Corky Froggett did not write many letters.

'*Dear Yvet,*' she read, '*I am sory I did not say goodby when I left the other day, but this leter will have to do instedd. With you I have shaired the best moaments of my life, but I canot let anything stand in the way of my loyelty to my imployers. I felled very bad when I reelised I had not been on hand when my young marster needed me. We will not meat agane. Tahnk you for evverything. Corky.*'

A tear threatened the hundred-per-cent perfection of Clothilde's *maquillage*.

The Earl of Hartlepool agreed to come down to London for his wedding. Though the Countess of Lytham St Annes assured Araminta that this was a demonstration of his love for her, the real reason he'd been persuaded to leave Little Tickling was that he was running out of matchsticks and had found a new supplier in Mayfair.

* * *

The Hunt Ball at Tawcester Towers passed off without incident. Blotto and Twinks were in sparkling form, their feelings being mainly ones of relief. The Countess of Lytham St Annes' machinations at Rules restaurant had let them both off the hook. Not only had the Earl of Hartlepool's marriage stopped Twinks from being lumbered with him, it had also mopped up Araminta as a potential fiancée for Blotto. Never had two jilted people been so happy.

They were equally happy some months later when it was announced, to general surprise, that Araminta, Countess of Hartlepool, was expecting a baby.

And when a boy arrived (as transparently pale as his mother), the happiness spread to Whiffler Tortington. As well as having married the woman he loved, he now achieved his only remaining ambition. He renounced his claim on the Hartlepool title, and happily endorsed his new half-brother as heir to Little Tickling and everything else.

His life was also enhanced by a generous allowance from the father who couldn't remember what he looked like. Frou-Frou kept lots of friends from her theatrical days and, the nights when Whiffler wasn't with his muffin-toasters at the Gren, there was nothing the couple liked better than going into the West End. To see the newest, hottest revue.

And in time, too, they became parents.

Barmy Evans and his men in black all received substantial prison sentences, which would prevent them from being a threat to the public for a long time to come. And Barmy's dangerous socialist plans were put in abeyance (for the time being).

Pierre Labouze and Everard Stoop, who had not in fact done anything criminal, continued to make a little money on the side from matching up superannuated showgirls with vacuous aristocrats. Dolly Diller, realising that she wasn't going to be spending much more time with Barmy

Evans, was happily married off to an Anglo-Irish Earl, who owned most of County Offaly.

When Everard Stoop, in the American Bar of the Savoy, announced that the union was 'an Offaly good thing', how his acolytes roared.

And, of course, Labouze and Stoop continued to produce intimate revues. In fact, on the night the heir to Little Tickling was born, they opened a new one, called *Light Up With Laughter*, whose opening number ran,

> 'When you're feeling low
> And you've had your go
> And there's nothing coming after . . .
> When your face is long,
> And you need a song
> That will echo to the rafter . . .
> When you feel like doom
> And you're sunk in gloom,
> You're in need of something dafter . . .
> So, come on, unwind –
> Yes, switch off your mind . . .
> And just Light Up With Laughter.'